DEAD DROP

EMMA ROSE WATTS

COASTAL PUBLISHING

Also By Emma Rose Watts

Dead Calm
Death Match
Death Blow
Dead Drop

Dedication

For my family.

Prologue

Franklin County, Florida

Death awaited but he was blissfully unaware. The occupant in the Ford truck flicked out a fourth cigarette into the blackness that swallowed everything. Hot embers bounced as it hit the ground. "C'mon, c'mon," the driver repeated, growing tired of waiting outside Ruby's Bar. It was a seedy shack on the edge of town that attracted the unfaithful and bottom feeders of society. The beer was cheap, and the women were easy but that's why that lowlife was there.

In the distance, a figure emerged from beneath the glow of the bar's doors, staggering, fumbling with keys as he headed over to his green sedan. Nick Hammond had his arm slung over some tramp who looked like she was three sheets to the wind. They both stumbled, and the driver heard them laugh.

The driver clenched the steering wheel tighter.

She wasn't meant to be with him. Oh well, collateral damage.

Everything would still go as planned. Nick made it to his sedan and opened the back door and motioned to the woman but for some reason she didn't want to get in. Who would? A moment of arguing back and forth and the woman slapped him across the face, turned and strode back to the bar.

For a second Nick looked as if he was going to follow but instead he opted to get into the driver's side. His overly expensive vehicle grumbled to life, kicking out a huge plume of white smoke before reversing out and taking off.

Perfect.

The driver in the truck smiled and waited a few seconds before following.

Nick headed north on Begonia Street before hanging a left onto US-98. He was heading home, home was Apalachicola. A few minutes' drive and he would pass over the Big Bend Scenic Byway. It was a long stretch of road that separated Eastpoint from Apalachicola — a connecting highway that cut through the bay. The occupant of the following truck knew the timing had to be just right. There couldn't be any mistakes. As they cut through pine forest and near unspoiled seashore, they passed several vehicles heading in the opposite direction. The driver of the truck swept the mirrors checking for vehicles from behind. There couldn't be any witnesses. The closer they got to the byway the more excited the driver became. The truck roared forward stealing the moment before it was gone. Flooring the gas pedal, the driver took off closing the gap between the truck and the green sedan. A few tense seconds then the truck slammed into the back of the sedan, causing it to swerve all over the road. Nick managed to get control of it, so the truck veered around the sedan as if to take over — just as the rear wheels aligned with the front of the truck, the driver yanked the steering wheel hard and collided with the car. A sudden clash of metal, sparks flying and a shattered taillight and the sedan spun out of control. Brakes screeched and the truck driver watched as Nick lost control, left the road and dropped over the edge, crashing down against the rocks and water.

The driver brought the truck to a crawl and looked out the rear window. The driver waited, searching for signs of life. Then, a door cracked open.

"Damn it!"

Nick was still alive. The driver watched him crawl out the side of the vehicle gripping his chest. The driver backed up the truck with the intention of finishing the job using a single round fired from a Glock laid on the passenger seat.

Just as the driver was about to get out and bring an end to his pitiful life, a set of headlights blinked into existence. A vehicle was approaching from behind and fast. There was no time to finish him. The driver banged a fist against the doorframe, hit the gas and took off at a high rate of speed.

Chapter 1

Skylar Reid shifted uncomfortably in her seat waiting for Sam Walker to emerge from the house. Ben, her psychiatrist and now close friend, had asked her to stay at his place for two nights to look after his thirteen-year-old son while he was away in Miami taking a course to update his skills. Of course she said yes but it was only after she agreed did she think it might have been a bad idea. She wasn't a mother. What on earth was going through his mind to ask her? She'd originally tried to wiggle her way out of it by telling him to contact Sam's grandmother who lived in Tallahassee but unfortunately she'd taken a nasty fall and was in no condition to be looking after a kid. She honked the horn for a third time and glanced at the clock. At this rate she was going to be late to the scene, all of which would give Harvey another reason to shine his knuckles.

Finally, Sam came out of the Mediterranean-style

home, one hand clutching a piece of toast, the other dragging a backpack. He was wearing a pair of sunglasses. He took after his father in the looks department. Good looking, blue eyes, swept-back hair and clothes that screamed they had money. While they looked alike, when it came to communication they were worlds apart. In the few hours she'd been there she had barely got a word out of him beyond yes, no, and it's over there when she asked for where things were in the house.

Sam hopped in and cut her a sideways glance.

"What took you so long?" Skylar asked as she threw the gearstick into drive and peeled out of there breaking a few speed limits in the short distance to Carrabelle High School. Instead of answering her question he glanced around the floor of her beat-up truck. "You know, you should really consider cleaning this up," he said. "It's a hazard."

"You sound like Harvey," she replied while keeping her eyes fixed ahead.

"Who's that?"

"My partner."

Sam took another bite of his toast and wiped some of the crumbs that fell on his leg onto the floor. As they drove in silence, Skylar looked at him.

"You know, you don't talk much," she said.

He shrugged. She noticed he was turned ever so slightly and leaning against the door as if trying to keep his distance from her. As he reached into his bag to get out a drink, he dropped his toast and well, anyone would have thought someone had cut his leg off or killed a pet. Out of nowhere he burst into tears. As he bent to scoop it up, Skylar noticed a dark circle behind his sunglasses.

She swerved to the side of the road, a few minutes away from the school.

"Hey, hey, it's okay. It's just toast."

He replied but she couldn't make out what he was saying through all the sobbing. Skylar reached over and placed a hand on him and the very second she did, he flinched.

"Sam. It's okay." He continued sobbing. "Do me a

favor, take your glasses off."

He shook his head, so she snatched them away from his face to reveal a large purple bruise around his left eye.

"What the heck? How did that happen?" she asked.

"I had an accident at school," he blurted out taking his sunglasses back from her and placing them on again. She recalled him coming in the previous afternoon and not saying a word to her. He'd retreated to his bedroom and only came out to collect his dinner and even then he was wearing sunglasses.

"How?"

"Does it matter?"

"Your father told me to look after you while he's away. Now he returns tomorrow and the last thing I want to do is hand you over with a black eye."

"I told you it was an accident, I fell over."

"Interesting. Were you wearing gloves at the time?" she asked looking down at his hands which didn't have a single mark on them. Skylar wished she hadn't said anything because after that he completely shut down. She peppered him with a few more questions but got nothing out of him. She would have pressed him for more information but a text came in from Harvey asking her where she was. She sighed, glanced at Sam and then pulled away heading for the school.

When they arrived and stopped outside, Sam was quick to hop out.

"So I'll pick you up—" Before she got the rest out he slammed the door and strode away into a crowd of students.

"Right," she said. Skylar took a quick second to text Harvey back to say she was on her way. They'd got a call early that morning of a jogger finding a dead body down by the Big Bend Scenic Byway. Harvey had already headed down there and was working with Hanson and Reznik to process the scene.

Just about to leave, Skylar glanced over to the school and saw three kids around the same age as Sam shove him into a door before walking off laughing. He dropped his bag and several of his books fell out. Skylar hopped out to go and give him a hand but before she crossed the road he'd already scooped them up and disappeared inside. Standing there with a hand on her hip and her thoughts far from her work, she couldn't help think back to her own school life. It wasn't easy. And the more awkward or quiet a child was, the greater the chance of being bullied.

She was starting to think that Sam wasn't telling her the complete truth.

* * *

Skylar ducked under the yellow crime scene tape that was looped around a few trees to prevent curious onlookers from getting too close. It was always the same. A small crowd would gather to gawk, and gossip. Harvey was on the phone when she arrived. Hanson was taking photos while Reznik and one other officer were getting statements from lingering bystanders. As she pitched sideways down the green embankment heading over to the large rocks that were positioned on either side of the road, Hanson noticed her.

"Glad you could pull yourself out of bed, Reid."

"Had to drop a kid off at school."

"A kid? I never took you for the mothering type. Did I miss the last nine months or have you adopted some poor soul?"

"Hilarious. What have we got?" she asked looking down at the body that was still covered.

"Forty-five years old, Nick Hammond, a local to the area of Franklin County. From what I've been able to glean it was some kind of hit and run." Hanson guided her around to the back of the vehicle. "We've got a smashed taillight, tire tracks all over the road up there and some red paint on the rear and side," he said pointing it out.

"So he died in the crash?"

"No, his body was found outside of the vehicle. While he had a nasty gash on the forehead it doesn't look like that's what killed him but we should know soon enough. My money is on internal injuries."

"Where's Jenna?"

"Haven't seen her but Harvey has contacted the ME

office."

Skylar walked back to the body just as Harvey ended his call.

"Reid, glad you could…"

"Don't even say it," she said cutting him off. "Already heard it from Hanson here." She pulled back the cover and took a look at the victim. Nick Hammond was around six feet tall, with a dark tan and horseshoe-shaped hair. He was dressed in a white shirt with two palm trees on the breast pocket. She took out her phone and took a quick snapshot of his face.

"My initial thought was robbery but there was a large amount of money still in his wallet, his gold wedding band and Rolex watch weren't taken so that rules that out."

"Anyone see anything?" she asked.

"Nothing. No reports last night of a crash. Though going on where the vehicle landed… at night it would have been hard to see it. Most folks would have driven right by it. A jogger this morning found the body around six."

"And you've had the body here this long?"

"You can't rush these things, Reid."

Skylar nodded getting up and walking over to the green Jaguar XJ sedan. It was a nice-looking car, high end, with black leather interior and all the trimmings. The airbag was deflated. There was a fine layer of white powder, which came from the airbag covering the seat, but beyond that there were no noticeable prints, which might have been visible because of the dust. The front end had smashed into the large boulders, preventing it from sinking into the bay. She reached into her jacket pocket and pulled out a pair of blue latex gloves and snapped them on before looking inside the vehicle for anything suspicious or out of place. Then she stepped back and walked around the vehicle. "So our victim gets knocked off the road, he survives, gets out of the vehicle and then drops. Nothing was taken, at least that we know of. So does anyone know where he was coming from?"

Reznik made his way over. "Found a receipt for Ruby's

Bar from last night in his wallet."

"All right, well I'll head over there to see what I can dig up, in the meantime, let's process those tire tracks, get in contact with his wife. Harvey, maybe you can head over there with me and deal with that."

"I handled the last one," Harvey said.

"What about the body?" Reznik said.

"Why are you asking me? Speak to Jenna, oh and check CCTV in the area."

"Cameras? Around here?"

"You'll be surprised at where folks have them nowadays," she said.

Reznik put a hand on his hip and shook his head in confusion before walking away. Skylar started climbing back up the embankment to her truck, her mind already lost in thought.

"Skylar!" Harvey said trying to catch up. He panted hard as he made it to the top. "Where were you this morning?"

"Dealing with Ben's kid." He gave her a confused

expression. "I've been taking care of him while Ben's away. He's in Miami at the moment and returns tomorrow."

She continued on to the truck. Several seagulls wheeled overhead screeching.

"Wait up. What's the hurry?" Harvey yelled.

She pulled open her door and hopped in, fired up the engine and brought the window down. "No hurry. I just have a few things I need to get done today before he gets back and well with all of this now on my plate…"

"Skylar?"

She sighed then blurted it out. "I think someone's bullying Sam."

"Sam?"

"Ben's kid. Come on, Harv, catch up." She put the gear into drive and kept her foot on the brake.

"Catch up? I don't have to remind you that…"

"Yes, yes. You were here first. Look, are you coming with me to Ruby's or not? We can talk to the family after that."

He thumbed over his shoulder. "Yeah, but I brought my SUV. I'll follow you."

Skylar pulled away before he could say any more. It wasn't like her to speed through a crime scene but then again she'd never been made responsible for someone else's kid. It also didn't help that she'd suffered through abuse at her own high school. It seemed to come with the territory when you were a cop's kid. Still it was all hitting a bit too close to home. As she drove the short distance to Ruby's Bar she thought back to those days. The afternoons she came home from school with no sneakers because they'd stolen them from her and cut them up, or the day she was sporting a cut lip and a shiner. Her father had torn into her like it was her problem. Everything was backwards in her home. When her mother wasn't drinking like a fish, her father was having a go at her. How she managed to rise out of the ashes of her past was a miracle in itself. She didn't want to see what had happened to her happen to anyone else, especially not Ben's kid.

Chapter 2

Ruby's Bar was a cesspool. Why a health inspector hadn't closed the place down was beyond strange. It was located halfway down Begonia Street. It was pushed back from the road, nestled into the surrounding pines and shrubs overlooking a small pond. The structure itself was made from bamboo and palm tree branches, and resembled one of the many tiki huts that could be found throughout Florida — except this place looked like a stack of cards just waiting to be blown down by the next hurricane.

Skylar didn't wait for Harvey to arrive. Heck, she didn't even see him in her rearview mirror when she drove away. Dealing with murders had become old hat to her. Even though most were solved in the fine details, the rest was routine, run-of-the-mill police procedure.

Outside there were several motorbikes parked, and tables full of sunburnt locals. Few tourists made it down here and those that did obviously hadn't read the reviews online or they had a death wish. It wasn't that the area was seedy but like any small town it didn't take much to draw in the wrong crowd. Skylar glanced at a dilapidated wooden sign that advertised twenty cent wings, and one dollar fifty beer. How on earth did they make a profit with that? She knew about loss leaders, all businesses had them but a dollar fifty for a beer? Was it beer or water? A few heavyset fellas with tattoos and sleeveless shirts gave her an unsavory glance as she made her way in. She wasn't sure if that was their way of checking her out or if it was because she stood out like a sore thumb in her suit jacket. Everyone in there was wearing the least amount of clothes possible. Some sweaty biker put his feet across the gangway as she tried to make her way to the bar.

"Excuse me," Skylar said.

"Excuse you?" he said in a joking manner to his three pals who were dressed in nothing more than cut-off shorts, flip flops and bandannas. Their skin was lobster red, and they had the remnants of zinc cream still on their noses which meant they were likely fishermen or just really particular about skin care. "Hey darlin', how about you sit on my lap and I'll buy you a drink?"

Skylar turned and smiled. "Tempting but I'll pass."

As quick as a flash he was up and in her face. "Oh don't be like that."

"Davis!" a voice bellowed from across the room. Both of them looked over to see a tall guy with slicked-back hair, wearing pants, well-polished shoes and a crisp shirt, shaking his head. The guy in front of Skylar stepped to one side and sneered allowing her free passage. Skylar flashed a smile and walked on up to the bar.

There was a gorgeous young gal, blond hair, dark eyes, wearing a bikini top with tight yoga pants, behind the bar. Skylar glanced down to the stranger who had intervened and gave a nod. He made a gesture back by raising his glass before returning to speaking with a long-legged woman beside him.

"Can I get you anything?"

"Who's that?" Skylar asked, nodding to the guy.

"That's Rich Brown. The owner."

Skylar pulled out her phone, and badge.

"Oh you'll want to speak to him," the bartender said.

"Actually I was hoping to speak with you. Were you on last night?"

"I was."

"Until?"

"Eleven."

"Do you remember this guy?" Skylar pulled up a photo of Nick on her phone.

She cocked her head sideways and glanced at it. "Yeah. Hard to forget a face like that. A real douche bag. He has come in here many times over the last couple of months. Always stays until the end and tries to pick up single girls. He never bothers to take off his ring. I mean, can you believe that?"

"Oh I've seen it," Skylar said, thinking back to the dating company that was operating in Carrabelle for a while until it was closed down due to numerous complaints. That had brought a smile to Harvey's face because Callum Jackson was funding the place and anytime he could bring him down a notch was a good day.

"Anyway, he looked drunk when he came in here. He ended up groping a few too many ladies' asses in here and Rich had one of our guys toss him out."

"So he left alone?"

"Not alone. I saw him walk off with Trish. How he managed to pull that off is beyond me but whatever he told her couldn't have been good as she returned a few minutes later cursing under her breath."

"Did she say what happened?"

"No, she grabbed up her stuff and left."

"You have a number for Trish?"

"We get a lot of customers, detective. I know some by name but that's it."

"So this Trish got a last name?"

"Dawson."

Skylar took down a few notes and thanked her. "So you said he would come on to women in here. Did he ever hit a home run or was striking out the norm?"

"He landed a few. Again, they must have had too much to drink or it must have been that money he was flashing around."

"Money?" Skylar asked.

"He offered to pay for all the drinks in the bar. It was his usual method. He would show up and buy a round for everyone in the house. From there he had women coming up to him all night hoping he was going to buy them drinks."

"And did he?"

"Of course." She pointed over to the corner where there was a booth. "He used to sit there and have us bring bottles over throughout the night. He ran up a large tab. Though he always paid at the end of the night, that's why Rich never had any problems with him. But he overstepped the line last night."

"In what way?"

She glanced over to Rich who was now looking at her.

"Look, it's probably best you go speak with the owner.

All I can tell you is that he was here and in my books he was a dirty old man who liked to hook up with twenty-year-olds. Hell, some of them were young enough to be his daughter."

"He has one?"

She shrugged. "It's a figure of speech."

"Right." Skylar tossed down a few coins for a cold drink and was about to head over to speak with Rich when Harvey came in. He spotted her from across the bar and stuck his hand up. She waited and he came over out of breath.

"You run here, Harv?" she asked with a smirk dancing on her face.

"No, but I nearly ended up in a fight out front."

"Three guys with no tops on?"

"Yeah."

She laughed and walked on toward Rich. "Mr. Brown, Franklin County Sheriff's Office. Can I get a moment of your time?"

He turned on his barstool and smiled. "By all means. I

always have time for Franklin's finest. Can I get you two a drink?"

Harvey looked as if he was about to say yes when Skylar replied, "Already have one."

"So what can I do for you?" Rich asked.

She showed him the face of Nick Hammond. "You familiar with him?"

"Nick. Yeah. Please tell me that photo is not what I think it is."

"I'm afraid so."

Rich sighed and shook his head. "I knew he'd eventually piss off the wrong guy."

"So you knew him well?"

"Listen, detective, anyone who comes into my bar and drops the kind of cash he did on a weekly basis was more than welcome. Heck, he spent more in one night here than most of these bums do in a week."

"So last night. What happened? Gal behind the bar told me that you had a little trouble."

"Oh he'd just had a few too many to drink. You have

to know what Rich was like. He liked to party."

"You knew he was married?"

"Of course. Listen, he shouldn't have been married and spending his weekends hooking up with single women here, but tell me how many people have you seen with money who are faithful?"

Skylar noticed the woman draped over Rich's shoulder, and the ring on his hand.

"Okay, so?" Skylar asked. Harvey took a seat and Skylar handed her drink to him. He sniffed it as if expecting to find alcohol. It was just orange juice.

"Like I said, we get all types showing up here. It can get rough at times. Nick would take offense to anyone who didn't treat him like the center of attention. We had a few new guys here last night. Gangbangers, I think you call them. Well he got slapped down by one of them. I had my guys break it up and toss them out."

"And this girl called Trish. What about her?"

"Trish Dawson is a dancer here at the bar."

Harvey looked around. "You're telling me all those

women on the dance floor aren't paying customers?"

"A busy house attracts customers, detective. I know you'd call it smoke and mirrors but I call it running a profit. I pay a few girls to dance here every day. It attracts in the single guys who go on to buy drinks, food and well, I think you get the picture."

Skylar continued her line of questioning. "So Nick comes on to one of your dancers."

"Yeah, groped her ass. Had it been anyone else he might have got a free pass. It's not like we are hard on rules in this place but the girls on the dance floor are off-limits. That's a no-no. I warned him on two occasions but he had way too much to drink."

"So he left with Trish."

"No, he was tossed out. I never saw him hook up with Trish after, that's news to me."

Skylar nodded a few times. "And what about this guy he was with?"

"I didn't know him. I remember him but I don't recall getting a name."

"Did he buy anything?"

"No. Nick buys everything. That's why people flocked around him."

Harvey piped up. "Okay so back up a bit. You mentioned he groped one of your dance girls and then he was tossed out and yet you said earlier that he was slapped down by one of these gangbangers, which one was it?"

He looked awkward and uncomfortable and if Skylar wasn't mistaken, she was beginning to think that he was lying.

"He got a slap down from this guy, it was broken up and both of them were tossed out. Nick came back about ten minutes later."

"And you let him in?" Skylar asked.

"Like I said, he was a paying customer."

"So was the other guy, which by the way raises questions. How did you know he was a gangbanger?"

"He'd been in on a few occasions. People gossip. Word gets around."

"Whose crew does he run with?" Harvey asked.

"I have no idea."

There was a long pause. Just the sound of music pulsating out of large speakers filled the void while scantily clad women swayed to the rhythm, attracting eyes from every corner of the room.

"Do you at least recall what this gangbanger looked like?"

"Bald, had a tattoo of a dragon on his neck. Sorry, I can't be much more help than that, however we do have CCTV."

Skylar pulled out a card and tossed it on the table. "Call me if he returns or you remember anything else." She turned to leave. "Oh, and one last thing. Beyond Nick spending money in here, did you ever speak to him?"

"Only when he stepped out of line which was quite often."

Before they left, Harvey said he wanted to get a copy of their surveillance footage from the previous night. Rich told them to come back in a few minutes.

* * *

Outside, Skylar and Harvey stood by their vehicles, glancing back at the bar.

"You think it's a member of the Latin Syndicate?"

"Possibly," Skylar said, her eyes scanning the crystal-clear waters.

"Skylar, if you don't mind me saying. You seem distracted. Like your heart's not in this. Are you sure you're okay?"

"Yeah, I'm fine."

"Because we can always let Hanson and Reznik handle this."

She shook her head. "No, I just need to get some sleep."

"You not sleeping?"

She reached inside her pocket and pulled out some pills that her doctor had prescribed. Skylar gave them a shake. "These help but they leave me feeling groggy."

"And not with it, I know. I used to take them," he said.

Her brow pinched. "You did?"

Harvey leaned up against her truck. "A year before you showed up here I got called out to a meth lab that was operating on the outskirts of town. Hanson and I were there. Reznik had the day off. And yes, I didn't enjoy having him as a partner for those few days. Anyway, this guy pops out of nowhere and opens fire. Hanson took a round to the back. Luckily he was wearing his vest. I froze. I don't know why. Had it not been for another officer who arrived a minute after us, I think I would have been dead."

"I don't get it. What happened?" Skylar asked.

"The shooter was just a kid. He was seventeen years of age." He paused looking into space as if he was reliving it in his mind. A few seconds later he shook his head. "Anyway, an officer from Carrabelle took him out. The kid died that night. After that I couldn't sleep for months. It kept replaying in my head. You know, over and over again."

"So how did you manage to get over it?"

"I didn't. Time eventually did its job and I got therapy."

"Are you telling me you went and saw a shrink?"

Harvey suddenly realized he'd said too much and he'd placed himself on the same level as her. For months he'd been acting like going to a shrink was for people who were mentally unstable and here he was pouring out his heart not realizing that he was no different than her. The fact was no matter how strong a person was, all of that could change in a heartbeat on the job. No training could prepare a person for it. Seeing a kid get blown away, or hearing your fiancé was killed on the job could damage anyone's psyche.

"Look, I'm gonna go get that recording from their CCTV then we'll head over and speak to the next of kin."

"Sure," Skylar said watching him walk away. There was so much that Harvey held back. There were moments she thought she knew him and other times she thought she was only scraping the surface.

Chapter 3

The call came in while Skylar was waiting for Harvey
to collect the footage. Skylar glanced down and looked at
the caller ID. It was Ben. She took a deep breath and
answered as she gazed out over calm waters.

"Ben. How's it going?"

"Good. Should have everything wrapped up by three
tomorrow afternoon and then I'll catch a flight back and
be home around six. How is he?"

"Sam?"

"I don't have another child."

"Right," she said. "Fine. I mean…"

"Okay, what did he do? Did he cover the toilet seat
with cellophane again? I told him not to do that but you
know how kids will be."

"No. He hasn't pulled any pranks." She shifted
uncomfortably trying to think about how to raise the
topic. She wasn't sure, to be honest, but based on what

she'd seen that morning and her own experience she thought it was best to just come out with it. "But eh…"

"Skylar. Just spit it out."

"I think he's being bullied."

"What?"

"I noticed he had a black eye this morning."

There was dead air on the phone, enough to cause Skylar to ask if he was still there. Ben was quick to reply. "I'm coming home."

"No, listen, Ben, I can handle this. You just focus on what you've got to do there."

"But…"

"Trust me."

He sighed. "Okay. Just don't go making it any worse."

"And how would I do that?"

He didn't reply to that, instead he said he had to go before hanging up.

Skylar chewed over what could be done. She hadn't dealt with bullying before and she'd seen the way her parents had dealt with it. Her father had told her to get thicker skin and her mother had asked her what she'd done to deserve it. Yeah, odd for sure but that was them to a tee. Right then there was a knock on the window. It startled her and she twisted to find Harvey there. After she brought her window down, Harvey raised up a flash drive. "Got the recording."

"You checked it out?"

"I was in there all of five minutes. What do you think?"

"Salty," Skylar replied.

"Anyway, I'll hand this off to Axl and see what he can find. We should head back to the station and you can jump in my vehicle."

"What about mine?"

He stepped back from it and eyed it like he was at a car wreck. "We'll go in mine." That was all he needed to say. "Anyway, you want to grab a coffee before we head out to see Ms. Hammond?"

"Vagabond?" Skylar asked.

He sucked in air. "Ooh, can't be doing that."

41

"Seriously, Harvey, Barb doesn't have spies."

"You'd be surprised at how quickly word gets around. Besides, shouldn't you swing by there and bury the hatchet with her?"

"I don't have any problem with her, she refused to serve me so as far as I'm concerned we are done. Life is too short for drama," Skylar said.

"Barb would beg to differ."

"Actually I think I'll just grab a coffee over in Apalachicola."

"Suit yourself."

He turned and headed over to his truck. "Harv, do you think I make situations worse?"

Harvey turned and his eyebrows rose. "Where did that come from?"

"Just curious."

He put a hand on his hip and eyed her like he was contemplating either telling her the truth or a lie.

"You know what. Forget the question," she said.

She brought her window up and peeled out of there

heading for the station.

* * *

Axl had always been a bit of a mystery figure to Skylar. Since joining the department she'd been told about him and had even spoken to him on the phone but to date she hadn't met him. When he wasn't helping the police he was working in his own business, which offered computer support and services. All she knew was he was African American, had dreadlocks and knew his way around technology like the back of his hand. Inside the station that morning it was busy. Phones ringing off the hook, officers tapping on keyboards and several of them dashing in and out of the building.

Fortunately Reznik and Hanson were nowhere to be seen. Skylar was about to make a phone call to the high school and see if she could arrange a time to speak with the principal when Captain Joe Davenport stuck his head out of his office and made a gesture.

"A moment, Reid."

She nodded, threw her bag down and headed in,

closing the door behind her as Harvey came into the main office.

"Take a seat."

"I'll stand if that's okay."

"Fine. How are things?"

"Good."

He nodded and leaned forward. His desk was immaculate. He suffered from a mild form of OCD so he tended to keep everything in place and if anyone picked up a framed photo or paperwork, he would readjust it to its original position. Davenport scooped up his coffee cup, which had the words I'm The Boss on the front.

"I was going over your file."

"My file?"

"Don't be alarmed, Reid. Everyone in this department has one. We like to make sure that things are ticking over nicely and the only way to do that is to keep track of how each of you are performing."

"And?"

He took a sip and flipped open a yellow folder in front

of him. It was thick, and full of papers. She glanced to the side of him and saw more folders with the names of officers, though most of them appeared to be a third of the thickness of hers.

"Things are good. A little rough around the edges but overall satisfying."

He leaned back in his chair. "But how are you feeling about it all?"

"About?"

"The arrangement. Working here. Your partner."

"Fine," Skylar said.

She knew to keep the conversation to a minimum. The less rope she offered, the less chance of Davenport hanging her with it, at least that's the way she looked at it.

"No complaints about Baker?"

"None. Why, has he been complaining about me?

He stifled a laugh. Obviously he must have been. Skylar frowned. "Sir, is there anything you wish to say?"

"No. I just wanted to check in on you. See how you were doing. We get so busy around here that we tend to overlook people and some folks can feel as though they are falling through the cracks." He paused. "Are you?"

"Am I what?"

"Falling through the cracks."

Okay, she had to admit the conversation was a little odd. Not once in the time she'd been working there had he pulled her in for anything other than to yell at Harvey and her over what they weren't doing, or could have done better, and now here he was acting like he was her pal.

She gazed down. "No, I think I'm good."

"It's just I was talking with Ben recently."

"Ben?" she asked with a look of confusion. She didn't like where this was heading.

"Walker."

"No, I know who you are referring to, I'm just wondering why you were chatting to him?"

"Well it's come to my attention from unnamed parties that we should be doing more for our frontline officers. You see so much and no one really asks you how it's affecting you. Then of course with the recent news about bullying in the workplace we just wanted to be sure that everyone was being heard."

"Things are fine. Thank you for asking. Captain, is Ben working with some of the officers here at the department?"

"He has for many years. Though of course it's been on a case by case basis."

"Meaning?"

"Meaning that it's confidential. The service is there if officers choose to use it. I'm just glad you have."

"Am I the only one?"

"No. Of course not. Heck, I even speak to him once a month. Though that's mostly to deal with the ongoing issues at home."

"Ongoing issues?"

He got this embarrassed look on his face and got up and closed the blinds to keep out prying eyes.

"My wife thinks I don't spend enough time with her."

"Really? And has Ben been able to help?"

"Yes and no. I mean, he knows his psych mumbo

jumbo like we know the law but it takes a woman to understand a woman, don't you think?"

"Possibly." Skylar got a sense that he was about to pepper her with questions and that the whole reason why she'd been brought in was to do with him and not her.

"Just out of curiosity. If someone upset you and then after sent you flowers to apologize, would you consider that bad?"

"Um." She paused to think about it. Certainly many guys had sent her flowers over the years but she couldn't think of a time when they'd done it in order to say they were sorry. "I think it would be okay."

"Exactly!" he said, stabbing the air and becoming all theatrical. "That's what I told her but would she take it that way? Nope."

"Well there is the other side of the coin," Skylar remarked.

"Side of the coin?"

"Well think about it from her perspective. You get into a fight, say a few words you don't mean and then a few hours later you bring her flowers. What message do you think that sends to her?"

"That I'm sorry. I messed up."

"Well that's obvious but now every time she looks at those flowers she's reminded of what you did wrong."

"What?"

"Yep," Skylar said.

Davenport frowned. "No. That's not right. Every time she would look at them she should be thinking… ah, what a sweet guy."

Skylar pursed her lips then replied, "Sorry, it doesn't work like that. Sure, that might work if you had done nothing wrong and it was her birthday or you just did it as a romantic gesture but when you throw an argument into the loop, women tend to deal with it differently."

He sighed and slumped down in his seat. "I swear as long as I live I don't think I will understand the opposite sex."

"Join the club," Skylar muttered.

"You'd think by now that we would have cracked the

code but all I seem to do is screw it up."

"What did you do?"

"Ah you don't want to know. The last thing I need is to have two women against me," he said before laughing. There was a long pause then he continued. "Okay, so I won't do that again but then what is the solution?"

Skylar smiled. "To be honest, captain, I think you should be speaking to Harvey. Now there's a guy who seems to have mastered the art of marriage. Myself? I'm liable to make the situation worse."

Davenport snorted and gestured towards the door. "Good talk, Reid."

＊ ＊ ＊

Harvey was chewing away on an apple when she closed the door behind her. He was hunched over someone looking at a computer screen. "Can you zoom in?"

"That's as far as it will go, mon! I would need more time to clean it up."

Skylar caught the thick Jamaican accent.

"Well this video is absolutely useless," Harvey said

stepping back to reveal Axl. Axl turned in his seat and smiled. "Ah, Skylar Reid. I've heard a lot about you. It's finally nice to put a face to the name."

"Likewise," she said extending a hand and shaking his.

He was a broad-shouldered guy, muscular, good-looking. He could have easily been a model. She'd always pictured him as some easygoing, beer-swigging layabout that just happened to have talked his way into a good position with the department, but it was clear from his clothing that he took pride in the way he looked. He wore pinstripe pants, a dark blue shirt, and multiple wristbands, and his smell? She caught a whiff of his cologne and it was out of this world. She wanted to ask him what it was but with them only having just met she figured it would have come across as slightly odd.

"You might want to get your partner here a cold drink. I think he's about to blow a blood vessel," Axl said.

Skylar laughed. "He's always like that."

"I am not!" Harvey said clenching the muscles in his jaw.

"Anyway, did the video reveal anything?" she asked.

Harvey tossed his apple core into the trash can. "Did it like hell. I swear the camera they were using in that bar must have been something bought from a dollar store. It's terribly grainy, in black and white and it kept cutting out. Plus they had positioned it behind the bar so all you could see was a few people at the bar and the rest can't be seen."

"I told him that's how they function over there. It's a shady place. Nothing good comes out of Ruby's Bar — except the wings. I have to admit, they sell decent wings. Strange really," Axl said leaning back in his chair. "I figured with their low prices they would drop the ball on the meat but it's the beer. That beer is like sucking dirty rainwater out of my eavestrough." Both of them gave him a confused look and he continued. "Not that I've ever tried that."

"So what does it tell us?"

"He was there. That's for sure and he certainly loved to grope. He got a nice right hand from one gal at the bar before he disappeared into the shadows," Axl said. "But that's it."

"What about our guy with the tattoo on his neck?"

"Nothing but I told Harvey here that I think it's a member of the Outlaws."

"The motorcycle gang?"

"Yeah. Look, I've been in Ruby's a number of times. For the wings, that is. Anyway on a few occasions I've seen some of these rough guys show up. They are all brawn. The owner has tossed them several times. They're always causing fights and whatnot. But I do recall one of them having a tattoo on the neck."

Skylar looked at Harvey. It was worth looking into. It wouldn't have been the first time that gangs had wandered into their neck of the woods. The Latin Syndicate was more common but bikers roared through Carrabelle on occasion, usually when they were making their way down to Miami.

"Anyway, we do have some good news," Harvey said. "The owner told me that Nick was a lawyer."

"What?"

"Yeah, I'm guessing you forgot to ask that."

"He said he didn't speak with him beyond a few times," Skylar said in her defense.

Harvey smiled as he headed over to the coffee vending machine and slotted a few coins inside. "Like I said, Reid, you really are dropping the ball. What is up with you lately? I swear you've got your head in the sand."

Axl looked at her and she shrugged. The fact was he was telling the truth. It wasn't just the whole thing with Ben's son getting bullied that was bothering her, it was the fact that her father had left a voice message. She hadn't seen him in several years and then out of the blue he thought he could just wiggle back into her life by asking her if it would be okay to visit. He was the last person she wanted in Carrabelle. She didn't want to think of all the damage he could do by simply opening his mouth.

Chapter 4

Harvey wanted to hear back from the ME before they approached the next of kin and declared it a murder. It was obvious another vehicle had been involved based on the findings of tire marks on the road and damage to the sedan, but Jenna would be able to shed some light on what had caused his death. In the meantime, Skylar was planning on running a few errands and then meeting up with him at the ME's office just after noon. She'd just pulled out of the parking lot when her phone jangled. She swerved off to the side of the road and took the call.

"Ms. Reid?" a woman asked.

"Yes?"

"This is Principal Myers, I'm going to need you to come to the school."

"Oh. Right. Of course." She ran a hand over her forehead. "What's up?"

"Probably best I tell you in person."

"I can be there in five minutes."

After hanging up she sat there for a second or two before taking off. This was really going to throw a wrench into the works. How did anyone manage their life with a kid? She'd been so excited about the prospect of having a child with Alex that she hadn't given much thought to the responsibility side of things. She felt like a fish out of water and it wasn't even her own. As her truck blew through the streets of Carrabelle she thought back to the first time her father had shown up at her school. As a busy police officer in New York he didn't take too kindly to being pulled away but with her mother not capable or incapacitated due to having drunk too much — a common daily occurrence — he didn't have much choice. The principal was insistent.

She recalled him showing up and getting into an argument with the principal and gripping her hand tightly as he led her out of the school. Once they were out of earshot of the principal he ripped into her. Telling her that she couldn't do this again. It was an inconvenience.

What he meant by that was she was an inconvenience. Of course had her mother been in the right state of mind she would have shown up and that would have been that. Instead, she was constantly knocking heads with him and feeling like a thorn in his side as she wrestled with growing up without her mother's support.

So much had changed between them since those days. Her father no longer drank. At least that's what he told her. Nine years of sobriety he'd said the last time they spoke. She didn't know whether to believe him or not and by the time she reached an age to make a clean break she didn't care one way or the other.

When Skylar arrived at the school, she killed the engine and headed inside, she made a beeline for the administration office that was close to the main doors. Inside, an older lady with specs was glancing at paperwork when she approached the front desk.

"I'm here to see the principal. Skylar Reid."

"Oh yes, if you want to take a seat over there, she'll be right out."

Skylar took a seat on a small chair and twisted one of the rings on her hand around. It was like being back in high school all over again. The nerves. The tension. The worry she felt and the lack of people to talk to. Fortunately enough, one of the staff in her school paid close attention and within a matter of days after the embarrassing confrontation her father had with the principal, Skylar found someone to confide in. She often wondered what happened to that teacher after she graduated. Did she ever really know the impact she'd had on her life?

Several minutes passed before a door off to the right of the cramped office opened and a young girl came out and shuffled out of the office with a grim look on her face. Skylar raised an eyebrow.

"Ms. Reid."

She turned to find an average-looking woman. She was neither tall, nor thin or overweight. Her hair was pulled back tight in a ponytail, and she wore thin-rimmed glasses. Like any true principal in command of a school, she conveyed an air of confidence as she made a gesture towards her office.

Skylar headed in and took a seat.

In front of her was a large mahogany table with a large desktop computer screen, a mouse and mouse pad, and a yellow cup full of pens. There was a gold nameplate on the front of her desk with the name Julia Myers.

She heard the door close behind her and then the principal took a seat.

"What relation are you to Sam?"

"Oh, I'm just doing a favor for Ben. We're friends."

"And where is Mr. Walker?"

Skylar frowned. "Away on training, he returns tomorrow evening."

She sighed. "Look, I'm not sure if I should be telling you this but Sam is absent."

"Absent? But I dropped him off at school today. I saw him walk in with my own two eyes."

"Well he never attended any of his classes."

"You have surveillance here, do you not?"

"We do and it's already been looked at. Not long after he walked in the main doors he went into the bathroom and then five minutes later he exited the school."

"Do you know where he is?" Skylar asked.

"That's what I was about to ask you," Julia said.

Skylar felt her stomach drop. This situation couldn't get much worse. Not only had she been placed in charge of Ben's son and he'd already got a black eye but now he was missing?

"Well, I have no clue."

"Right." Julia turned towards her computer and moved the mouse ever so slightly. "Today isn't the first time he's gone missing. He was absent on Monday, Wednesday and of course today."

"Why didn't you phone?"

"I did. I left a message on the voicemail. I gather no one has heard that?"

Skylar nodded. "Right, well look, leave it with me. I will track him down. He couldn't have gone far. I have a good feeling I know where he is."

"Good. Okay. And would you have a contact number for Mr. Walker?"

"I do but if you don't mind I would like to deal with this matter."

"Because he's placed you in charge?"

"Exactly."

Julia rose from her seat and walked over to the window and looked out. She clasped her hands behind her back looking as if she was about to give some grand lecture. "Please be aware that this is a very serious matter."

"I understand."

She turned. "Then I hope to hear from you shortly. Regardless, I will be speaking with Mr. Walker when he returns."

Skylar got up and was about to leave when she turned and faced her. "Tell me, Ms. Myers. Has Sam ever been to see you about being bullied?"

She squinted and shook her head. "No. Never."

"And none of the teachers have noticed?"

"Ms. Reid. Our teachers do the best job they can

under the circumstances. Not everything that goes on in this school can be caught but if you're suggesting what I think you are, we will definitely look into it."

Skylar gave a nod and then exited. There was very little she could say. Often victims of bullies didn't say anything out of fear of being victimized again. Logically going to a teacher would have been the best thing to do but it often resulted in further trouble. She knew all too well how that happened.

Outside, the air was thick and humid as she made her way over to her vehicle. As soon as she got inside she turned it on and cranked the air conditioning high. She sat there for a few minutes tapping her fingers against the steering wheel before setting off for Ben's home a few streets away. Instead of pulling into the long driveway that wound up to his house, she parked a short distance away and crossed through the thick pine trees and shrubs making her way up to the house. The last thing she wanted was for him to hear her approach. As she traipsed through the dense forest surrounding his home she swatted at a couple of mosquitoes that were feasting on the back of her neck. She still hadn't got used to them. When she came out on the other side she crept around the back of the house making sure to stay quiet. She reached the sunroom door and pried it open. From the moment she cracked it open she heard music playing. It wasn't the regular type but the kind heard by someone playing a computer game. Skylar slipped off her shoes and padded through the sunroom into the kitchen and made her way to the staircase. She'd made it up three steps when it creaked loudly. Within seconds the music turned off and she heard shuffling. She smiled and shook her head. Not bothering to remain in stealth mode she made her way up and pushed open the door on Sam's room. The controller for his PlayStation was on the floor, as was his school bag. She walked over to his closet and pulled it open and there looking up at her was Sam.

Skylar dropped down and crossed her legs.

Sam didn't say anything at first.

"I..."

"How long have they been bullying you?" Skylar asked.

He frowned as if expecting her to tear into him and give him a lecture.

"Several months."

"And you haven't told your father?"

"No. He wouldn't understand. He would just show up at the school and that wouldn't get me anywhere except another beating."

"Why are they beating on you?" she asked.

He shrugged. "I don't know." He sniffed a little. There were no tears but his nose was runny. "Maybe..." he trailed off and went quiet.

"Maybe?" she probed for more details.

Sam was hesitant to reply but when he did he dropped his chin slightly. "I spoke to this girl."

Skylar smiled. "What's her name?"

"Chloe. Chloe Warren."

His face lit up.

"And?"

"She used to date this guy, Kirk Bowman." He sighed. "I thought they were over. I mean, if you ask her she would say they were but Bowman has some major issues with that. According to him she's still his property."

"Property? No woman is a man's property."

"Exactly, that's what I told him... right before he punched me." He rolled his lip below his teeth. "Anyway, after that I haven't been able to make it through an entire day without him and his goons jumping me."

She nodded. "What's this Chloe girl look like?"

His face lit up. "Flaming red hair, dark eyes. A real..."

"Babe?"

That got a smile out of him. It also reminded Skylar of the girl she'd seen in the principal's office. Had she been in to speak to her about Kirk?

"Anyway, she probably thinks I'm a real loser now."

"Uh, I wouldn't be so quick to come to that conclusion."

"You don't know how it works at the school."

She nodded. "The principal left a voice message. Did

you delete it?"

He nodded. Skylar stood up. "Come on."

"I'm not going back there."

"I didn't say you were. I want to show you something."

Sam's brow pinched before he got up and followed Skylar out of his room and down the stairs. She scooped up a pillow from the sofa and led him out into the backyard after slipping back into her boots. It was warm Florida day and the sun was high in the blue sky with hardly a cloud in sight.

"What are we doing?" he asked.

"There are a few ways to deal with bullying. Usually it's best to speak up but sometimes that only gets you so far." She held out the pillow. "Take a swing at this."

He stifled a chuckle. "Are you kidding me?"

"Go on."

He stood there for a second or two and then threw a right jab. She moved it out of the way before he could hit it. "Okay, you're pretty slow."

"If you're going to insult me, I..." he said before walking away.

"Sam. Hold up," she said calling him back. She tossed the pillow on the ground. "How big is this Kirk guy?"

"Imagine Goliath."

"Right. So pretty big."

He pursed his lips together and nodded.

"So you've got speed and size working against you. In which case you need to use that to your advantage."

"What do you mean?"

"Life gives you tools to deal with challenges. You wouldn't use a hammer for a job that doesn't require a hammer. The same applies for dealing with those who attack. It's not all about punching and kicking. It's about using this," she said tapping the side of his temple. "Who knows what Kirk's deal is? But one thing for sure is he knows what to expect with you, so you need to throw him off his game."

"You want me to punch him?"

"No, he'll take care of that. You're just going to use his

energy against himself."

"Okay, you have me confused."

"Throw that punch again."

"But…"

"Just throw it."

He gritted his teeth for a second. "Don't say I didn't warn you." When he threw the punch she sidestepped and trapped his arm and moved forward knocking him off his balance. She did it gently enough not to hurt him but fast enough that he couldn't react. Once he landed, she grabbed his hand and pulled him back up. "You see how much effort I exerted?"

"Yeah, but I'm a kid."

"It doesn't matter. It's the principle. For every action in life there is a reaction. You have a split second to decide what that reaction will be. You can cower back, you can take it on the chin, or you can learn how to flow with it and use it to your own advantage. You understand?"

He nodded slowly. "I think."

Over the course of the next hour she led him through five different moves that he could learn that would enable him to react to the most common attacks. She hadn't learned these things from her time in the police, even though they had given her basic martial arts training. She'd gleaned them from her father. It was probably the only thing that he'd taught her that had been of any use.

She watched as Sam slowly but surely grasped the concepts. He was blown away when she showed him how easy it was for him to take her down with the least amount of effort. She saw a spark of confidence return to his eyes and then she dropped the last lesson on him.

"It's all about practice, and repetition. Now remember, you're only to use this when pushed into a corner. I don't want you heading into school and antagonizing this Kirk guy, okay?"

He smiled. "Man, I can't wait to show this to dad."

She wrapped an arm around him and ruffled his thick dark hair as they headed back in. For the first time since arriving she felt the wall between them crumble.

Chapter 5

After a quick phone call to the school to make sure they were updated on the situation, Skylar made her way back to the department to meet up with Harvey. The next order of business was to notify the next of kin. It was never pleasant.

"Where did you disappear to?"

"Had to head to the school to deal with a matter related to Sam," Skylar said in a relaxed manner as she looked out across the glistening waters. There were several boats out bobbing along, and the sun was reflecting off the surface causing her to squint. She dropped her sunglasses down and got comfy in the passenger seat of Harvey's SUV.

"You mind putting your feet down? I just got this thing detailed."

She smirked and shot him a sideways glance. He had this look of concentration on his face as if he was running through what he was going to say to the victim's wife. She'd often hear him muttering under his breath, almost rehearsing it. She'd brought it up one day in conversation and asked why he did that? After being a cop for so long it should have become old hat. Nope. Not him. He liked to be on the ball and that meant making sure he didn't put his foot in his mouth — part of the reason why he preferred to tell the loved ones what had happened instead of Skylar.

"By the way, what did you say to Davenport?" Harvey asked.

"Why?"

"He pulled me into his office and wanted advice on his marriage. He said you told him that I was a master when it came to marriage."

"Well you are," she replied not even looking at him and admiring the view. That was one thing she had got used to since moving away from New York. The view was spectacular along the Forgotten Coast. Although it couldn't beat the atmosphere and buzz found in the Big

Apple, it had grown on her and it was beginning to feel like home.

"Well I don't appreciate it."

"Oh c'mon, Harv. You love to be the center of the attention and you're always harping on about how great your marriage is. It was a compliment."

He went quiet for a few seconds. "I appreciate that but my marriage is far from perfect. It might seem that way on the surface but believe me, Elizabeth and I have our issues."

"Like?"

"I'd prefer to not go into it."

"Aha, in the bedroom, eh?" She chuckled.

"Why do you immediately assume there is some intimacy issue?"

"You're getting on in years. It happens."

"I'll have you know I hear nothing but praise from Elizabeth when it comes to the bedroom."

"Sure you do," she said.

"What's that supposed to mean?"

"Women tell you what they want you to hear."

He frowned and looked ahead then back at her. "Okay, now you are getting me paranoid."

"Oh I'm sure in your case everything is just fine."

The rest of the journey was spent in silence.

Nick Hanson had lived in a gorgeous white clapboard home that overlooked the bay just off Bay Avenue. It was a two-story Victorian home set back from the road and surrounded by palm trees and an immaculate lawn. When they pulled into the driveway there were two gardeners hard at work trimming the hedges. The smell of fresh-cut grass filled the air as Harvey killed the engine and they hopped out. A woman who had to be in her early thirties emerged from the door with a tray of iced tea. She had short dark hair, and an excessive amount of makeup. She was wearing a T-shirt that was far too tight for her thin frame.

"Oh boys, come and get it," she said eyeing the two buff-looking gardeners who were both not wearing shirts and flaunting their tanned bodies.

The second she caught sight of Skylar her brow pinched.

"Can I help you?"

Harvey was quick to reply, pulling out his badge and flashing it. "Franklin County Sheriff's Office."

She gave a concerned look, made a gesture to the hedge trimmers and waved them on through the open doors. Inside the home they walked on down a rosewood hallway through to a large living room that was filled with white leather seating. It looked like something out of a home and décor magazine. There was a white area rug beneath a thick mahogany table, a large floor-to-ceiling bookcase packed with hardcover fiction and at the center of the room was a skylight that let in a warm band of summer light down to the table in the middle of the room. A large bouquet of red roses was on the table and Skylar noticed a small envelope and card off to the side.

"Is this about Nick?"

Skylar took a seat, Harvey remained standing as he gave her the news. "Mrs. Hammond, I'm afraid your husband was found deceased this morning."

They watched her expression. There was a lot that could be gleaned from the way a person reacted upon hearing of their loved one's death. Every person was different. Some would collapse, others sob gently, others would pepper them with questions but in this case Mrs. Hammond did neither, she smiled.

Harvey tossed Skylar a look. He didn't need to say anything, she knew what he was thinking. It was odd. Very odd.

"I knew it would happen. I told him. Heck, many people told him but would he listen? Nope. That's just like Nick. Always liked to push the envelope and see how far it could get him. Can I get you some coffee?'

"Mrs. Hammond."

"Call me Nancy."

"Nancy. I don't mean to sound insensitive but you don't appear very cut up by the news."

She turned to head out but glanced back for a second. "Why would I? He was a pig. Everyone that knew him said he was, and after living with him for the past year we were close to calling it quits."

She walked out without giving it a second thought, leaving them wondering how someone could be so cold and callous. Not satisfied with her answer, Harvey followed her into the kitchen. Skylar waited a second or two then headed in to join them.

"Yes, he came home for supper then went out again."

"Why?"

"He tends to work very late but he always comes home for his dinner."

"And what do you for a living?" Skylar asked.

"I'm a hairdresser."

"And your husband was a lawyer."

"That's right," she said as she went about making some coffee. The kitchen was modern, state-of-the-art with top-of-the-line stoves, fridges and dishwasher. There was a large breakfast counter in the middle of the room with a two-piece sink.

"Were you aware of him cheating on you?"

"Of course. It was no mystery."

"And yet you decided to stay in the marriage?"

Nancy poured out two cups of coffee and slid them across the granite counter towards them along with milk and sugar. "Detectives, our marriage wasn't great from the beginning but we made it work." She eyed the ring on Harvey's hand. "I'm sure you can relate, yes?"

Harvey didn't respond to that but instead threw back another question.

"Where were you last night?"

"Here. I finished work at five, went out for a drink with a friend and was home by six."

"Does this friend have a name?"

"My boss, David Manning. Would you like his phone number?"

"Was it just the two of you?"

"It was."

"Are you in the habit of going out for drinks with David?"

She smiled, leaned against the counter and took a sip

of her coffee. "Ah, I see where you are going with this. You assume because I tell you that our marriage wasn't all fireworks and rainbows, and that I went out for a drink with my boss that I'm maybe somehow behind his death, is that right?"

"Not exactly," Harvey said. "But you'd have to admit your response to being told that your husband is dead is a little strange."

"Maybe. But if you knew my husband you might not find it so strange." She paused for a second. "Listen. Our marriage wasn't exactly what you call normal but then what marriage is?"

"So you had some kind of arrangement?"

"Call it what you will. It worked and when things were good they were really good."

She walked over to the counter and pulled out a box of cookies, shook them onto a plate and offered them to Harvey. He glanced down and politely declined. She offered them to Skylar and she scooped up four in one go. "Do these have macadamia nuts in them?"

DEAD DROP

"That's right."

"God, I love macadamia nuts. It's that crunch and yet at the same time the softness. It's so…"

"Divine," Nancy said with a smile forming on her face.

Skylar stabbed the air. "Exactly!"

Harvey gave a disapproving look and Skylar returned to dipping a cookie in her coffee.

"So Mrs. Hammond."

"Nancy."

"Right. Nancy. Do you know of anyone who might have wanted your husband dead?"

"He was a lawyer, and a damned good one at that. There were hundreds of people he bumped heads with. Getting threats came with the territory."

"He never mentioned anyone in particular?"

"If he did I wasn't listening. What you have to understand is when he came home he was either pissed about a case he was working on or drunk. I got used to tuning out what didn't apply to me. As long as his supper was on the table along with a glass of scotch he was

79

happy."

"So you turned your eye to what you didn't want to accept?" Skylar asked taking a bite of a cookie and glancing over at her.

"Yes."

"And is there anyone who can verify you were here last night?"

"I phoned a friend of mine, Debbie Jones. I'll get you her number."

"And could we get the number for your boss too? Thanks," Harvey said as she walked out of the room to retrieve it. As soon as she was gone Skylar walked around and grabbed up another cookie.

"Really?" Harvey said.

"You need to relax a little, Harv," she said. Nancy returned and handed over the phone numbers. Harvey stepped out the rear door into the sunshine to call them.

"So will you be keeping the place?" Skylar asked.

"Of course, this is mine."

"Oh you own it."

"Yes. Oh what, because I'm a hairdresser I don't have financial sense?"

"I didn't say that."

"But you assumed it."

"Okay, fair enough."

"Actually to be honest the place was my father's. After he died it was passed on to me. Along with a sizable inheritance."

Skylar nodded slowly before taking another sip of her coffee. "So money has never been an issue?"

"Not for me."

"Your husband?" Skylar asked.

Nancy snorted. "He earned exceptional money but blew through it like water."

"His money or yours?"

"Both." She pursed her lips together and folded her arms. Her demeanor changed and Skylar picked up on it.

"I imagine that would have been a point of contention."

"Like I said, our marriage wasn't a bed of roses,

detective."

"Were you aware of how much money he was spending down at Ruby's Bar?"

"Oh so that's where he was hanging out?" she asked.

Skylar frowned. "You didn't know where he was?"

"Oh I knew he wasn't at work. At the end of the evening he would turn his cell off. The only way I knew that he was seeing other women was because I found selfies on his phone, along with a video."

"Sex video?"

"Something like that."

Skylar nodded and placed her cup down. "Did you ever bring it up?"

"Didn't need to."

Right then Harvey returned placing his phone back into his jacket pocket. "Well it appears your alibi is solid, at least for now. Debbie said she would be right over to be with you. That's it for now. Nick's body is currently at the medical examiner's office while they finish up their report. We'll get in contact if we have any further questions."

They were led outside. Nancy didn't remain on the porch. Instead she thanked them for stopping by, scooped up the empty glasses outside and went in. As they walked back to the SUV Harvey glanced at Skylar and she gave him the same look.

"That was odd," Skylar said.

"You're telling me. But it's obvious Nick was her sugar daddy."

Skylar shook her head. "I'm not exactly sure about that."

"Come on. Look at the place and all the money he spent down at Ruby's."

"Looks can be deceiving," Skylar said as she hopped into the passenger side. Harvey stood there for a second looking at her through the window and then hopped in.

"Am I missing something?"

Skylar eyed the two men cutting the hedges and then the house. She was sure she saw Nancy standing at the window for a second. The drapes moved ever so slightly.

83

"It's possible that all that money he was blowing was hers."

She brought him up to speed on what Nancy had told her as they pulled out of there heading back to the station. As they made their way across Big Bend Scenic Byway Harvey started spitting out potential ideas of how Nick reached his demise.

"Okay so he's spending all her money, he's seeing other women, so she follows him to the bar and waits until he leaves knowing that he was usually intoxicated and then she drives him off the road?"

"Possible though highly unlikely."

"So she pays someone else to do it. You saw the way she was eyeing those two gardeners like candy. Maybe she got fed up with him blowing through her inheritance and decided to nip it in the bud before Nick drove them into the poorhouse."

Skylar shrugged. Unlike Harvey who liked to think out aloud and throw out scenario after scenario no matter how ludicrous they were, she preferred to chew it over in her mind.

"Anyway, how did you get on with the ME?" Skylar asked.

"Ah, yes," he said. "I didn't make much progress. Jenna wasn't there."

"What do you mean?"

"There was some intern in there and let's just say he was more than a little green. Yeah, apparently Jenna has been off for the past few days."

"Is that so?"

"No, I was just saying it for the heck of it. What's up with you, Skylar?"

"Ah, Jenna's been having issues with her boyfriend. At least, that's what I think. I think he's been knocking her around but she won't admit it. Last time I saw her she had a mark on her wrist. She wouldn't say how it occurred but—"

"When were you going to tell me?"

"These matters are sensitive."

"Why didn't we just go arrest his ass?"

"If he is involved, I'll do it immediately but right now it's a little complicated."

Harvey snorted. "No, women are," he said.

Skylar chuckled. "Yeah probably best you don't say that around Elizabeth or she's liable to clock you around the head. Anyway, I'm gonna swing by there this afternoon and see what's going on. Listen, I think we should see what we can dig up about the Outlaws."

"Oh okay, let me get my little black book out. How do you suppose we do that? It's not like we have a contact on the streets."

"Oh but we do." She glanced at him.

"No. No. I am not going there."

"Harvey, from what we've been able to glean from our run-ins with him, he has his finger on the pulse in Franklin County. If anyone is going to know if they were involved it's him."

"I'm not going to speak to Callum Jackson," Harvey said.

Chapter 6

"Detective, how wonderful to hear your voice," Callum Jackson said. Harvey gripped the phone a little tighter. As strange as it might sound, Skylar's train of thought wasn't far wrong. Over the past few months Callum had been stepping forward and offering his services to the department. Although Harvey didn't trust him as far as he could throw him, he'd come through for them on three occasions with information that led to the arrest of drug and child traffickers in the area. Now Harvey was a smart man, he knew that Callum wasn't sharing information with the cops out of the goodness of his heart. He was a businessman, a crooked one at that with ties to drug trafficking that had stemmed back to the '80s. He portrayed himself as a pillar in the community but behind it all he was hiding his own dark secrets. No, these tip-offs had been nothing more than a means of getting rid of competition.

"I wish I could say the same," Harvey replied.

"Oh, I feel hurt," Callum said in his most sarcastic tone.

"Please understand I'm not calling you because I like you or wish to shoot the breeze. I wouldn't be doing this unless I felt it was absolutely necessary."

"Of course not. How can I help you?"

"The Outlaws. You heard about them?"

"You know the rule, don't you, officer?"

There was a short pause.

"No but I'm sure you're going to tell me."

"I can't discuss matters related to gangs over the phone. Only in person."

"Then how about you head on down to the station? I'll put the coffee on," Harvey said in his own sarcastic manner.

"Would love to but I'm actually babysitting my granddaughter."

"You. Babysitting?"

"Detective. I know you see me as this thorn in your

side but I have a life outside of my work. Just as you do, and family means everything to me."

"And that's why many of them are locked up."

He snorted. "Look, I would love to chat but…" He must have held the phone to his chest as his words became muffled. "Anna, darling, be careful. Don't go near the water."

He came back on the line. "If you wish to discuss the Outlaws meet me down at the harbor. I'm having coffee at Vagabond."

"Vagabond?"

"Yes, is there a problem with that?" Callum asked.

"Well. Can't we meet at the Carrabelle Junction?"

"No, detective. I like the coffee here."

Harvey grumbled under his breath.

"Fine. I'll be there in five minutes." He hung up and sat there for a second thinking it over. This was not good. Not good at all. This went against everything he'd been harping on at Skylar about. If Barb got wind of him schmoozing with her competition it could mean the end of freebies on Fridays at the Junction. And damn did he love those iced caps with the extra whipped cream on top.

Then again, how would she know? She was too busy running her store and any local with a lick of sense didn't go near Vagabond. He would get in and out. Make it quick. Find out what he needed from Jackson and then be out of there before anyone knew.

* * *

Ten minutes later Harvey killed the engine outside the Vagabond and sat in his SUV eyeing the crowds of tourists. He wanted to make sure there was no one there that he knew before he ventured in. Get a grip, Harvey told himself. Maybe Skylar was right. Maybe he was acting a little paranoid about Barb having eyes in the back of her head. Perhaps he'd spent too long listening to the stories of her knowing what went on in Carrabelle. He pushed out of his vehicle and made his way down the dock. Outside the air was humid. He pulled at his tie to get some relief from the heat. He kept his head down and darted into the café. The second he entered, Donny Wu yelled out his usual greeting. "Hello. How are you? Welcome to Vagabond!"

Harvey didn't make eye contact and quickly scanned the room searching for Jackson. Seeing that he wasn't there, he headed back out to the tables and chairs that were set up for those choosing to drink outside. That's when he spotted him. He was around the rear of the café, close to the water's edge. He was just about to head over when he felt a tug on his arm.

"Detective Baker. I thought it was you."

His stomach sank.

He turned to find Pete Welding, a local fisherman who was often seen inside the Carrabelle Junction.

"Hi Pete. What are you doing here?

"It's lunch time. I was about to head to Carrabelle for a bite to eat." He glanced at the Vagabond. "I didn't know you came here."

"I don't," he said quickly in his defense as if Barb herself was asking the question. "No, just searching for someone. Actually he's over there."

"Ah, right. Well I'll let Barb know I saw you."

"Actually if you don't mind, I'd like you to keep it under your hat. You know how these things are. She might get the wrong idea."

Pete made this O shape with his mouth like a guppy fish. "Oh, got you. Mum's the word!" he said before tapping the side of his nose.

"Besides, I don't even like the coffee here," Harvey said.

"Me neither."

Right then Donnie Wu emerged from the doorway. "Detective. I thought it was you. I just poured out your favorite. You still take it without sugar, yes?" Donnie handed it over and Pete's eyes bounced between them. Before he could say anything Pete walked away. "Good to see you, Pete," Donnie said.

He didn't reply. "Oh great. Now that's really done it," Harvey said.

"What has?" Donnie said following his gaze towards Pete who was now getting into his truck and eying

Harvey like a cheated lover.

Harvey sighed. "You ever have one of those days, Donnie, where you just think the world is working overtime to humble you?"

"Can't say I have but there is an ancient proverb that says... Arrogance invites ruin; humility receives benefits."

With that said he turned and walked back inside the café leaving Harvey contemplating it. Not wishing to waste any more time he headed around the back of the café and down to the outside patio that overlooked the boats.

Callum Jackson was dressed in a light cream-colored suit, white shirt partially undone, and dark brown shoes. He was sipping on coffee as Harvey came up behind him. Every time he was around the man he had this urge to strangle him. It might have been because he believed he was to blame for his sister's murder but in all honesty he just didn't like the guy. He gave off this creepy, snake oil salesman kind of vibe that made him feel as if he was trying to sell him a used vehicle.

Without even turning he greeted him.

"Detective. I thought I smelled the aroma of your cologne. What is that, Hugo Boss?

"It is," Harvey said pulling out a chair and taking a seat beside him. Callum turned and smiled. He had aviator shades on. He'd grown a mustache since the last time he'd seen him. It didn't suit him and on any other day he might have been inclined to tell him but he thought he would heed the words of Donnie and try to remain humble. Perhaps humility would get him a lead, and right now that was all that mattered.

"Have you met my granddaughter Anna?" he asked motioning to a little girl who was licking an ice cream and watching the boats come in. She had curly blond hair and reminded Harvey of Shirley Temple. Beside her was one of Callum's two bodyguards; the other was looming over Callum. He would deny that was what they were but they went everywhere with him. Two hulking men that looked as if they could snap a person in two just with a sneer.

"It's amazing how quickly they grow up, isn't it?"

"Yeah," Harvey replied.

"You have two children, don't you, detective?"

"I'd prefer if you didn't speak about them."

He removed his aviator sunglasses. "Business then. How can I help you?"

"A car accident over on the bend between Eastpoint and…"

"I know about it."

"What can you tell me?"

"Nick Hammond. Now that's an interesting guy. A little loose with his money but a damn fine lawyer. He will be missed."

"Were the Outlaws behind it?"

"The Outlaws?"

"It's come to our attention that Hammond might have had a run-in with one of them. A guy with a dragon tattoo on the side of the neck. You familiar with this individual?"

"If you're enquiring if they were responsible for the death of Hammond, I can neither confirm nor deny. I knew they were in the area conducting a little business but that's all."

"What kind of business?"

He chuckled and brought the cup up to his lips to take another sip. "The unsavory kind. What do you think, detective? Is there any other business they deal in?"

"You tell me. You're the one with your fingers in illegal activities."

"Come now, detective, let's not make accusations or bite the hand that feeds you. My life is an open book."

Harvey resented having to come to him. It was so demeaning.

"So you don't think they were behind the murder?"

He shook his head and placed his cup back down. "No. It's too sloppy. Not their style. Your man would have likely been found with a bullet to the head or not found at all. These guys don't knock a vehicle off the road then leave him to die. They enjoy the thrill of the kill."

"Do you?" Harvey asked.

Callum looked at him but didn't respond. Harvey

knew Callum was responsible for multiple murders, he just couldn't prove it. The man was as slippery as a snake. His ability to fly under the radar and get around the law had made him infamous in Franklin. Strong family ties, connections with lawyers, mayors and people in power gave him the leeway to operate with little interruption from law enforcement. On the few times Harvey had come close to pinning a crime on him, he'd managed to weasel his way out with large sums of money. The fact was it was going to take one huge mistake to take him down and unfortunately Callum wasn't in the habit of making mistakes, at least not ones that could be linked back to him.

"Anna. Come on now. Time to go." He turned back to Harvey. "Well I'm afraid I have to cut this short but I have enjoyed our little conversation. Maybe next time we can do this out at my home. Perhaps I could invite out your lovely wife and children?"

There was always a sense that he was threatening him in a subtle way. He didn't care about Harvey's family or spending time with him. He just wanted to make it clear that he was in control. It was all about control.

"But we were just getting warmed up," Harvey said.

Callum rose. "If you need to know more about the Outlaws I would suggest speaking with Keith White, the owner of White's Video Production in Carrabelle."

"What's his connection?"

"Have a good day, detective."

And just like that he was gone. Harvey remained there chewing over the information he'd given him and wondering whether it was accurate or liable to send him on a wild goose chase.

* * *

Jenna Madden lived in Carrabelle Cove Apartments just off Gray Avenue. It was a quiet nook that had a good reputation. The apartments themselves weren't much to look at — cream-colored clapboard siding, light gray shingles. She'd got herself a place there after taking over the position of chief ME from Ted Sampson. Skylar knocked on the door and looked around as she waited.

Two kids were on tricycles being chased by a young mother who looked like she hadn't slept in a month. The door cracked open ever so slightly, the chain hung loosely. It was Jenna.

"Hey, Jenna."

"This is not a good time, Skylar," she said peeking out.

"Everything okay?"

"It's fine. I've just got a stomach bug."

Skylar put forward a bag. "I brought you some soup. Thought you could use it."

Jenna glanced down at it. "Thanks," she said and reached out and took it. As she did, a part of her face that was hidden could now be seen.

"Jenna. Your face."

"Look, just leave me alone," she said then backtracked. "I mean. Thank you for bringing this but I really need to go lay down."

"Jenna."

"I just had a fall."

Before she could say any more Jenna closed the door.

Skylar stood there for a few seconds contemplating what to do. She pressed an ear up to the door but couldn't hear anything. Slowly she made her way back to her truck. When she reached it she turned around and made a beeline for the door. She banged a few times hard on it. Jenna opened the door again and Skylar told her to open up.

"But—"

"Just open the door or I'll send Harvey over and you know how he is."

She sighed and unlatched the chain. Jenna stepped back and Skylar stepped in. The lighting was low inside so it was hard to see her face clearly but she could tell it was bruised on one side. They ventured into the living room where the curtains were drawn and the TV was on playing some afternoon talk show. Jenna turned her face away but Skylar reached for her chin and twisted it around.

"He did this, didn't he?"

"No. Skylar, I don't want…"

Skylar moved across the room and pulled the curtains wide. Light flooded in and with it the truth of Jenna's situation. Not only was her lip busted up, and she was sporting one hell of a shiner, but the coffee table in front of her furniture was littered with crushed beer cans, empty bottles of bourbon and takeout food.

"Jenna. This is crazy. This has to stop. It ends today."

"It's nothing. I just took a fall."

"Yeah, then why do your hands have no grazes?"

Jenna sighed.

"Where is he?"

"He went out to get more booze."

"So he's out of work but he can afford to buy booze?" she scoffed. She understood being down on luck and trying to cope with alcohol, as she handled her own problems in a similar way but she knew her cut-off point — some didn't.

"Right, well I'll wait here until he gets back," she said about to plunk herself down in a chair.

"No, you need to go. If he sees you here, he'll—"

"He'll do what, Jenna? Huh?"

Right then she heard a truck pull up outside, and the clinking of bottles in a bag followed shortly after by a key being inserted into the door.

Chapter 7

"Who the hell is blocking our parking spot?" Darryl Harlow said as he slammed the door behind him. She heard him trudge down the corridor cursing under his breath. Skylar had never met him so she was curious to see Jenna's taste in men. Darryl rounded the corner into the living room and frowned. "Who the hell are you?"

"The driver of the vehicle that is taking up your parking spot," Skylar said.

Darryl was wearing a muscle T-shirt, a thick leather jacket with the collar pulled up, a pair of ripped jeans and large combat boots. His hair was dark and hung low past his shoulders. Certainly wasn't the kind of man she expected Jenna would date but then again her taste for wild colors and excessive makeup would lead anyone to believe she was into life on the edge. She still hadn't got the background on how she met him and after the way he'd treated Jenna she wasn't interested in knowing.

His eyes bounced between them and he placed down the bag of drinks. Jenna stepped forward, a bag of nerves, and made a gesture to Skylar.

"Darryl, this is Skylar, she works for the police department."

"The police?"

"We work together."

"You didn't tell me you were inviting anyone over."

"I didn't. She dropped off some soup."

He looked at her unconvinced. Skylar knew he was probably connecting the dots in his head and thinking that perhaps Jenna had called her to discuss abuse.

Darryl pulled a face. "Yeah well, nice to meet you but we have a lot to do today so if you don't mind," he said, stepping to one side as if to indicate that it was time for her to leave. When Skylar didn't move, Jenna spoke up.

"She's a guest."

"I understand and don't take this the wrong way but this is really not a good time."

Skylar was about to pipe up when Jenna said, "She's

staying."

Darryl flashed her a look of death. "Jenna. A word with you in the kitchen."

He turned and marched out. Jenna glanced at Skylar with pursed lips and followed him. Skylar waited listening to the conversation. He wasn't exactly trying his best to keep his voice down.

"I want her out of here now."

Surprisingly, Jenna began to stick up for herself.

"She'll go when I say so."

"Is that so?"

"Yeah. I pay for this apartment. In fact I pay for everything," Jenna said.

"And I told you that once I get a job again things will change."

"That was seven months ago."

"It's tough out there."

"You turned down three job offers."

"Working at some fast food joint?"

"It's a job."

"Yeah, I'd like to see you do that."

Skylar peered into the bag and looked at the alcohol. There had to be over fifty bucks' worth.

"Then go back to college and get trained."

"And how do you expect me to do that?"

"It might help if you didn't sit around drinking all day."

"Careful," he said.

"You know, Darryl. I'm getting tired of all the excuses you keep making. Meanwhile I'm paying for you to drink yourself into an early grave. Well it stops today. I want you out of here."

"What?"

"You heard. Gone. I want you to move out. And while you're at it, I want the keys to my vehicle back."

"You can't do that."

"I can and I have."

Skylar smiled. Although she knew that Jenna had let this issue with her boyfriend go too far, perhaps showing up here had been a good thing after all. Maybe the realization that someone else knew and that it was no longer a secret was enough to snap her out of whatever hold Darryl had over her.

"You know things can get real difficult, Jenna."

"Get out."

He laughed. "Yeah, acting all big because your cop buddy is here. Let's see how you are this evening when she's gone. You'll come creeping back. Begging me to return."

Skylar stepped out into the hallway and looked down towards the kitchen. Darryl had his finger in Jenna's face. He glanced at Skylar and then pushed past Jenna and made his way back to the living room. He scooped up the bag of alcohol and brushed past Skylar on the way out. The walls shook as he slammed the door.

Jenna appeared in the doorway of the kitchen, tears rolling down her face.

"You know I can arrest him right now and you can press charges."

"I don't want to, he didn't do it," she said as Skylar

made her way into the kitchen and put the kettle on to make some tea. Jenna slumped down onto a chair at the kitchen table and put her head in her hands.

"Jenna. I know you probably don't want to hear it but there are far better men out there in this world who will treat you better. I know you think he's only doing this because he's out of work but that is no excuse to hit a woman."

"He's a good guy, just a little lost."

"That's what a lot of women say about men who lash out at them."

"He didn't lash out."

"Oh c'mon, Jenna. I didn't just graduate from the academy. Good men don't hit women. It's as simple as that. They can make excuses all day long about the drink made them do it but that's just a cop-out for accepting responsibility for their actions."

She nodded. "I just…"

"Don't want to be alone?" Skylar said walking over and taking a seat across from her. She placed her hand on top of Jenna's as she nodded. "Join the club. But I would rather live alone than under the thumb of a tyrant."

"Was Alex a tyrant?"

"Alex? No, he was one of the good ones," Skylar said getting this faraway look in her eye. "But I dated my fair share of numbskulls before I came across him. And there is someone good for you out there." Skylar squeezed her hand.

Jenna nodded and pulled a few tissues from a box to wipe her eyes. "You miss him?"

"Every day," Skylar said. "But enough about me. You know he's probably going to show up here tonight. Why don't you go stay with your mother or better still stay over at my place tonight?"

"Thanks, Skylar, but no, I'm not going to be driven out of my own place. I don't want to be afraid anymore. I'm tired of it." She looked at her for a second. "I just wish I'd told him sooner."

"It's not easy."

"No it's not," Jenna said.

Skylar glanced at the clock. She needed to get back to work and find out what Harvey had managed to dig up. "You going to be okay?"

"Yeah. Thanks for coming by."

"Look, I really think I should bring him into the station. These things can escalate."

"It won't. Like I told you. He didn't do it."

Skylar couldn't believe she was covering for him but it often happened in domestic violence. More times than not it didn't end well either.

"If he shows up again, don't let him in and just phone the station or me."

"I will do."

* * *

Harvey was typing away at his computer when Skylar walked into the office. He glanced over the monitor at her then leaned back in his chair. "Well I managed to get a lead from Jackson."

"I told you."

"Yeah. Well don't get your hopes up yet. I tried

contacting Keith White and it appears his business, White's Video Production, is shut down. It hasn't been in operation for over two months and according to his mother she hasn't seen him in over a month."

"Well that's not good."

"So we are back to square one."

"Curious though, did you take her word for it or did you drop around and see for yourself?" Skylar asked.

"Well I…"

"You just phoned."

He nodded.

Skylar perched on the edge of his desk. "And Callum didn't give you any more than that?"

"Nope. You should have seen his face. The smug little asshole thinks he's above the law. I can't wait to finally put the nail in the coffin and put him away."

"All in good time," Skylar said patting him on the chest. "Listen, unless there is anyone else that we can speak to today, I'm going to knock off early. Sam is at home and I don't want him to be alone."

"He's thirteen."

"And dealing with a lot of issues right now."

Harvey smiled. "It feels good, doesn't it?"

She turned on her way out the door. "What does?"

"To have someone else's problems to deal with besides your own."

She nodded. "I guess so."

"By the way, how did you get on with Jenna?"

"She kicked her guy out."

"Really?"

"No I just said it for the heck of it," Skylar said in a joking manner. She winked and headed out the door. On the way back to Ben's home she was passing through town and decided to swing by White's Video Production. It was located on the southwest side of town not far from the Marathon gas station on Avenue A. It backed onto Carrabelle Harbor. Skylar swung her truck into a parking lot across the street and sat there with the engine idling. White's Video Production operated out of a run-down one-story building that was made from weathered wood.

The only thing that didn't look like it was about to crumble was the roof, which was steel. Outside there were two large flower pots with dead flowers inside, and an American flag flapping in the breeze.

Skylar cranked up the air conditioning and waited to see if anyone would show. Multiple vehicles drove by, several stopped at a seafood shop across the street and there was a good amount of pedestrians but no one entered the video production store which had a closed sign hanging in the window. Ten minutes, then thirty minutes passed and Skylar decided that no one was there so she made a decision to head out. As she pulled out of the lot and was about to hang a right, she glanced across the street and swore she saw movement inside the darkened store. Were her eyes playing tricks on her?

A car behind her honked to get her to move. Making a quick decision, she headed across the street and parked outside White's store. She pushed out of the vehicle and approached the front, cupped a hand over her brow and peered in. It was dark and the pane of glass was dusty.

Nothing. She wandered around the side until she reached the back. That's when she noticed the rear door was open, and someone was inside clanging around. She glanced down the small steps that led away from the rear to a dock, and a twenty-foot fishing boat. Skylar made her way around. Just as she entered a man with a goatee was coming out. The second he saw her he dropped a large crate of video equipment in his hand and bolted.

"Hey!" Skylar yelled. "Police. Stop!"

The stranger darted to the front of the store and within seconds he was out and racing around the east side. Skylar wasn't that far behind. The stranger climbed over a chain-link fence and bounced off some stacked pallets then darted down the dock heading for the boat. Skylar yelled several times for him to stop but either he was deaf or he wasn't listening. The guy tossed several boxes used by fishermen behind him to try and slow her down but she hopped over them like an Olympic hurdler. Moving fast as he could he unwound the rope from a post that moored the boat and hopped in. The motor fired up but before he could give the boat some throttle, Skylar raced down the dock and launched herself onto the stern. She landed hard and slammed into him forcing him up against the wheel of the boat.

"Get off me," he cried out.

"Let me guess. Keith White?"

"And? Who are you?"

"Franklin County Police."

"Ah man. I haven't done anything wrong."

"Yeah? Then why were you running?"

"I thought you were with them."

"Them?"

"The Outlaws."

Skylar held on to him and gave him a confused look. "Do I look like a biker?"

"Do I look like a video production expert?" he shot back.

She pulled a face. "Shut the engine off."

Skylar stepped back and let him turn it off before they exited the boat and she led him up to his building. "Am I under arrest?" he asked.

"You want to tell me why your business has been shut for over two months now? And do you know your mother is looking for you?"

"Looking for me?"

Skylar looked at him and then raised an eyebrow before pushing him down onto a chair outside the rear of the store. "She lied, didn't she? You're staying with her."

"No. Hell no! It's just she hasn't been interested in where I've been in years. What did she say?"

"Where does your mother live?"

"On the east side of Carrabelle," he replied.

"So why are you running from the Outlaws?" she asked leaning up against a post and keeping a good eye on him.

"It's a long story."

"Yeah, well I'm all ears," Skylar said. Keith groaned and looked down at his feet. He reached down and picked up a few loose stones and tossed them down the steps.

"I owe them money."

"For what?"

He waved to the building, when she didn't connect the dots he clarified. "I borrowed money from them to get my business off the ground. We worked out a deal where they gave me a loan in exchange for payback over three years along with offering them free services anytime they needed it."

"Why would a motorcycle gang be interested in a video production service?"

"Look, shouldn't I get a lawyer or something?"

"Interesting. You have one?"

"Of course. Everyone does."

"Let me guess, your lawyer wouldn't by any chance be Nick Hammond, would it?"

He got this confused look on his face. "Yeah. That's my lawyer."

"Was your lawyer," Skylar said.

"What?"

"We found Nick's dead body this morning. He'd been run off the road."

A look of shock washed over Keith. He stared toward his boat. "Oh no. No."

"Oh no what?"

"I've got to get out of here." He bounced up and pressed forward only to be stopped by Skylar. She pushed him back but he came forward again. This time she took a firm grip on his collar and drove him back into the chair causing the whole thing to nearly topple over.

"Sit down!" She stabbed the air in front of his face with her index finger.

"You don't understand."

"Well then how about you explain."

Keith blew out his cheeks. "The Outlaws have their hands in a lot of businesses. I needed a loan to get my business up and running and the bank wouldn't give it to me. I sought out a few local loan places but they wouldn't touch me because of my bad credit history. Then I got chatting to this guy in a bar here in town who told me about a small loan company operating out of Miami. They said they approved everyone and with my skills in video production they would probably work out some kind of deal."

"This guy you met got a name?"

"I don't remember. I drank a lot that night."

"So?"

"I went down there and chatted to them and they loaned me the money. In exchange for a good interest rate they wanted me to do a few favors for them. You might want to call it undercover work. So they wanted me to video a few individuals, record some footage and whatnot."

"And you didn't think to question that?"

"I needed the money. Seemed like a fair exchange."

"The Outlaws wanted you to do this?"

"Not them specifically. I didn't know I was getting involved with them. If I knew that, I would have gone to someone else. No, it seems they are the ones that fund the loans behind this company."

"What's the name of the company?"

"Rapid Loans."

Chapter 8

Harvey was biting into a sandwich and doing research on the Outlaws when Skylar came into the office with a guy in handcuffs. "Skylar?"

"Keith White. I thought it was best you heard the story from him while I speak to Axl and see what I can dig up on a loan company operating out of Miami."

Davenport stuck his head out of his office and Keith used the opportunity to his advantage. "Hey I want to file a civil lawsuit against this woman. She manhandled me, and busted up my lip."

"You shouldn't have tried to run," she said handing him off to Harvey. Harvey led him away into an interview room while Davenport had a word with Skylar. The interview room was going through a renovation after an outburst by a guy they'd brought in to question. He smashed the one-way mirror and they were still waiting on the company to come in and fix it. Fortunately it was supposed to be done later that day.

"Man, what kind of sloppy operation are you guys running down here?" Keith said as Harvey sat him in a seat.

"Just take a seat and be quiet."

"You know I have rights. I'm entitled to a lawyer."

"And you'll get one soon enough."

Harvey headed back out and knocked on Davenport's door.

"Come in," Davenport replied.

"Sorry to bother you, captain." He looked at Skylar. "You want to tell me what's going on with him?"

"Didn't you ask?"

"I'm asking you."

"Harvey, don't stand in the doorway, come in." Davenport said waving him in. Harvey took a seat beside Skylar.

"That's our mystery man. The one that was arguing with Nick Hammond on the night he died. Says he was close friends with Nick and that he'd brought some questionable footage to Nick because he feared for his life and wanted to make sure he had something in place just in case anything happened to him."

"By who?"

"The Outlaws."

"I'm not sure I follow."

Skylar turned in her seat. "Apparently. It might not be true. Keith went to get a loan from a place called Rapid Loans in Miami. The company is run by a man named Bo Gonzales. Apparently the money for loans is funded by the Outlaws — he wasn't aware of this — and if anyone doesn't pay they get a visit. Well it seems that Keith was falling behind on his payments. Now because they wouldn't give him more time to pay he tried going the blackmail route and turned the tables on Bo Gonzales by recording him having an affair with some woman."

"To buy himself some time?" Harvey asked.

"Exactly. Except he didn't tell Bo this. No, he handed this footage off to our victim for safekeeping just in case anything happened to him while he tried to negotiate with Bo on his loan repayments. Makes sense, right? Well he trusted the wrong person. Nick showed it to Bo's wife and used it in court to land her a sweet settlement. It destroyed his marriage and crippled his business."

"So what happens to everyone who owed Rapid Loans money?"

"Well that's the interesting part. It appears Bo's wife worked for the company. After watching the video, she deleted all the files of those who owed money to get back at Bo."

"Nothing like the scorn of a woman!" Harvey ran a hand over his head. "I hope he made backups."

"Seems not. Apparently Bo is now flying under the radar to avoid the Outlaws."

"Because it's their money," Harvey said.

"Exactly."

"Probably dirty money too." Harvey cupped his jaw in his hand and tapped his lips with a finger. "I still don't get it though. So if the Rapid Loans database is wiped, how did they know about Keith?"

"Through Bo. Seriously, Harvey, are you not paying attention?" Davenport said.

"Lately I don't think he is," Skylar said half jokingly.

"Hilarious. Look. I'm trying to understand this. Keith takes out a loan and starts falling back on his payments. Fearing for his life he records a video of Bo cheating on his wife and uses it as leverage in order to not pay back what he owed?"

"Something like that, according to Keith he just wanted more time. He says he was going to pay them back. Was he? Who knows? What we are being told is that he gave that footage to the wrong person. Nick saw an opportunity and apparently made a good chunk of change from Bo's wife by being her lawyer and helping her win in court."

"So are you saying that our man in there is responsible for the murder because of what Nick did with that footage or are you saying that Bo or one of the Outlaws is responsible for Nick's death?"

"It could be any one of the three. Though my money

is on Bo. I've got Hanson and Reznik trying to track him down as we speak. Hopefully Miami police can locate him."

"If the Outlaws can't I doubt our boys in blue will."

"Ah you'd be surprised at how resourceful they are," Davenport said.

Harvey scowled. "So what's Keith's alibi for the night of the murder?"

"He says he was there at the bar and yes he got into an argument but it was over the footage being released without his permission. He was unaware that Nick had handed it over to Bo's wife until Keith learned that Bo was looking for him."

"So how did he wiggle his way out of that?"

"He made a run for it. That's why his business has been closed for two months. He's been trying to stay off the grid and one step ahead of Bo."

Harvey groaned. "Crazy the lengths people will go."

"You bet," Skylar replied.

"But on the night he was there, right?"

"Yeah, apparently he blamed Nick for ruining his life. It got a little heated and then he left the bar."

"And yet he's been on the run for the past two months," Harvey said. "So no one can verify his alibi."

"That's why I brought him in. I thought you might be able to work your magic on him, maybe find out if he doubled back and killed him."

Harvey got up. "So what now?"

"Turn in for the day. If we hear any more we'll keep you updated," Davenport said. "I'll have one of the other officers question him."

"Why? I'll do it," Harvey said.

"Harvey, you've been in since early this morning," Davenport said. "Go home. Get some rest."

"I'm fine."

"That wasn't a question," Davenport said.

Harvey gritted his teeth got up and exited with Skylar in his shadow.

"Hold up, Harvey."

Without looking at her he blurted out, "Why didn't

you tell me you were going to head over to Keith's place?"

"Does it matter? We got him."

"Yeah and I looked like a fool."

She shook her head. "Why?"

"Because I should have gone over there. I told Davenport that he wasn't around."

"You need to calm down," Skylar said. "We're partners. Sometimes you do one thing, sometimes I do another. Maybe he wasn't there when you phoned. And besides Davenport is just looking out for your well-being."

"I'm glad someone is."

Harvey headed off towards the interview room leaving Skylar in the main office, mouth agape.

* * *

Skylar had spent long enough working alongside him to know when to leave him be. Lately he'd been a little high strung and for the life of her she couldn't figure out why. It wasn't like they were in some kind of competition. She was just used to taking initiative. That's what they were paid to do. Worn out from the heat of the day and with Sam on her mind she headed off home hoping that tomorrow would give them something substantial to follow up on.

Skylar hopped into her truck and fired it up then pulled out of the parking lot. As the truck weaved through the roads, she heard an EMT siren's wail and a few seconds later an ambulance sped past her heading in the opposite direction. She glanced in her rearview mirror at it but continued on home.

When she arrived home that evening, Sam was watching TV and she noticed the light was flashing on the phone to indicate there were two messages on the answering machine.

"How we doing, Sam?"

"Good."

"You up for pizza tonight?"

"Sure."

She scooped up the phone and checked the messages. They were both from Ben and by the tone of his voice he was pissed. "Skylar. Call me."

Skylar kicked off her boots and headed into the kitchen. She fished around in the fridge for a beer and twisted off the cap. She made a quick phone call to the pizza shop to have them deliver a large pizza and then she took a seat at the breakfast counter and made the call to Ben.

"You called?" she asked.

"Anything you wish to tell me?"

"Oh I spoke with the school about the bullying. They'll look into it but they weren't aware."

"And?"

She knew what he was leading to but she wasn't sure how he knew. She'd made a promise to Sam not to tell his dad but it didn't look like she was going to be able to keep that promise.

"And look, I don't want you to blow your top but..."

"He's been skipping school. I know. I spoke with the principal today."

"How did she get your number?"

"That's right, you didn't give it to her even though she asked for it."

"I thought I could deal with it. You have enough on your plate as it is."

"My kid goes missing from school and you didn't contact me, Skylar."

"Because I found him and I didn't want to worry you."

She heard him sigh. "Well I am worried. Is he okay? Why did he leave? What's going on?"

"It's related to the bullying."

"Well that's obvious but why hasn't he told me?"

"Maybe because he knew you would react this way."

"React? How else am I meant to react when I find out my kid's being bullied and has been skipping school?"

"Look, I handled it. It's fine. He'll be there tomorrow."

"You didn't take him back in?" he asked.

"School's out. It's the evening, and no I didn't. Would you want to put him back into that environment straight away? He can't run from his problems," Skylar said.

"No, and he can't deal with them with the same mindset."

There was a pause as Skylar contemplated what he said.

"Look, in the future I would just appreciate it if you would let me know what's going on with my son, especially when I'm away from home."

"I would imagine after this you wouldn't entrust me with your son again."

He chuckled. "You're always ready for rejection, aren't you, Skylar?" He waited for an answer but she didn't give it. "Look, I'll be home tomorrow evening. If anything happens tomorrow please call me."

"You have my word."

He made a groaning noise before hanging up as if frustrated with being so far away. Ben had a good situation going for him. He worked from home, he was only ten minutes away from Sam's school and other than a trip to update his skills once a year he was rarely apart from Sam. It was a good situation but not exactly healthy.

It was probably the reason he hadn't dated. Skylar took a sip on her beer and headed into the living room to check on Sam. He glanced at her.

"What you watching?"

"*Enter the Dragon.*"

She laughed. "You pick up any new moves?"

He went red in the face as if he was embarrassed by the question.

"Are you sleeping with my dad?" he blurted out. Skylar nearly spat out her beer.

"Um. No but if I was I'm not sure that would be any of your business, young man." She tried to put on a mothering tone as if she even knew what that sounded like.

"But you like him, yeah?"

She was hesitant to respond but before she could, Sam continued, "Because he likes you."

"Does he?" she asked taking a seat and thinking this would be a good opportunity to get the inside scoop on what was going on inside his mind. Sam scooped out a few chips from a half-empty bag of Cheetos and stuffed them in his mouth.

"Oh yeah, he talks about you all the time."

She smiled. "Well he is my shrink."

"No, that night he went out for a meal with you he had this cheesy smile on his face for two days after that. I haven't seen him that happy since…" He trailed off and she knew he was thinking about his mother. She wanted to ask him about her but at the same time realized it was a delicate subject. Ben's wife had passed away six years prior in a skiing accident.

"He said you lost someone. Your husband," Sam said.

"Fiancé. And I didn't know he shared that with you."

"Oh he doesn't usually. He's very anal about what he can and can't say, and the only reason he told me that was he was planning on inviting you around for dinner and he didn't want me to open my mouth and say the wrong thing."

"Like bringing up the topic of my dead fiancé?"

"Yeah, something like that."

She couldn't help but find the humor in that. He continued watching Bruce Lee taking on twenty guys. Sam's head bobbed around like he was a part of the scene.

"Yeah, that's right. I lost someone close," Skylar said.

"Do you miss him?"

"Of course. I'm sure you miss your mother."

He was fishing into his bag when he stopped watching the TV and looked across to a photo on the mantel. It was a photo of them all together as a family. "Every day," he replied and then returned to chomping on the chips, though more slowly, more mindful as if trying to forget.

Skylar leaned back in the recliner and was about to get comfy when there was a knock at the door. Sam bounced out of his seat and answered the door. "Pizza," he yelled.

She got up to fish out some money to pay, then realized she didn't have any cash. "Oh, um. Do you take credit cards?"

"We do."

The pizza guy fished into his bag and pulled out a swipe machine.

"Technology. Gotta love it."

The pizza guy jabbed his finger at the device. "Oh and that button there is for the tip."

Skylar smiled and gave him a good tip before closing the door and scooping up a slice out of the box. Back in the living room she slumped down in the chair and looked over at Sam. She could get used to this. It certainly beat coming home to an empty boat. Skylar had taken a couple of bites of her pizza when the phone rang.

"Sam, do you mind grabbing that?"

He hopped up and returned a moment later. "It's for you. A guy named Harvey."

"Ah right, yeah, pass it here."

He handed it over. "If you're calling to go for a beer, can't do it. But we have a lot of pizza here."

"Actually, Skylar. I have some bad news."

"What?"

"Jenna is in the hospital."

Chapter 9

Skylar was in a daze as Harvey explained. Apparently not long after leaving her apartment Darryl had returned in a drunken state and forced his way inside and taken out his anger on Jenna. Skylar bundled Sam into the back of her truck and tore through the streets of Carrabelle heading for George E. Weems Memorial Hospital.

"Where are we going?"

"A friend of mine has been injured, just stay close," she said gripping the steering wheel tight as they pulled into the parking lot. This was the downside to having to look after someone else's kid. She was beginning to understand the demands and great responsibility that came with raising a child. The place was lit up and several ambulances were outside with EMTs assisting in emergency patients on stretchers. Skylar had never liked visiting hospitals. Just being around the sick made her want to break out in hives. There was something very cold to the place. She recalled spending many a night down at the hospital because her mother had drunk herself into a stupor and taken a handful of pills in an attempt to end her life. She'd sit in the waiting room trying to keep herself busy while her father would speak with doctors. In her mind she knew eventually her mother would die, she didn't expect it would be from suicide.

The main entrance doors hissed open and she kept a tight grip on Sam's hand as she made her way to the front desk to enquire about Jenna. She didn't have to wait there long as she spotted Harvey making his way down the corridor.

"Harvey."

He glanced at Sam but didn't look like he was in the mood for small talk.

"Skylar, I need to talk to you."

"Sure, but is she okay?"

"She's stable and will recover but..." He motioned towards a quiet waiting area further down the hall and led the way. Skylar tried to get more details out of him as to whether or not they had Darryl in custody but he didn't bother answering her.

"Sam, you want to go in there? I'll be right back, okay?"

He nodded and went back to looking at his phone as he went into a divided waiting room. Skylar could see him through the window as Harvey closed the door. He paced a little and scratched his head as if he was trying to figure out what to say.

"I spoke with several of Jenna's neighbors tonight and one of them said that she'd seen Jenna a couple of times with bruises on her. So we know this has been going on a while."

"Yeah it has."

He glanced at her.

"Why didn't you bring him in today, Skylar?"

Her brow pinched, a look of confusion. "What?"

"You went over there. You could have stopped this from happening. You knew this was happening and yet you did nothing?"

"Hold on a minute. Back up the truck. You know how it works with abuse victims. Not all of them will admit it and few want to press charges. Jenna didn't want me interfering. She said she could handle it."

"And you know that this is a part of the cycle of domestic violence. Even if the victim doesn't want to press charges, the state can still move ahead with prosecution. We don't know what kind of threats or intimidation he was using to keep her quiet. Skylar, you know you have to arrest someone on any domestic call. Once they make that 911 call to report a domestic the couple has lost control over their relationship for a while. She might drop the DV charges but it's in our hands from there."

Skylar stabbed the air with her finger. "I wasn't responding to a 911 call. And Jenna refused to admit that it was him. She only alluded to it."

"Well it was pretty damn obvious. We still could have filed some charges."

"Yeah well best of luck with that."

Harvey looked angered by her reply. He jabbed his finger down the hall and headed off making it clear that he wanted her to follow him. She had to practically jog to keep up. They went about six rooms down and then he opened a door. There was a nurse inside hunched over the bed. She turned and that's when Skylar got a glance at Jenna. She was hooked up with tubes and her face had been beaten so badly that she could barely recognize her. The nurse was tending to her wounds and Jenna didn't appear to be awake.

"Luck has nothing to do with it. Look at her." Skylar turned her face away. "Look at her!" Harvey said loudly causing several of the orderlies in the hall to turn and stare. Skylar looked back and tears welled up in her eyes.

"I'm sorry for intruding," Harvey said pulling the door closed. He turned towards her. "It's a little late for tears now. Davenport wants to speak to you." With that said he turned and walked away without saying another word. Skylar stood there not knowing what to say or do. She had dealt with abuse cases before back in New York and more often than not the victim would go to the station give a statement and then at the last minute decide they didn't want to press charges. In nearly all cases when the victim didn't want to appear for trial, the prosecutor would subpoena the victim. If they still refused to show, the prosecutor could continue with the trial or try and prove it based on statements given.

Skylar returned to the waiting room and motioned for Sam to follow her.

"Is that it? Are we going?" he asked as he tried to keep up.

"Yes we're going."

"How's your friend?"

"Sam, enough," she snapped out of frustration. He stood there staring at her, a look of confusion spread across his face. "Look, I'm sorry, I'd just rather not talk about it."

The journey home that night was spent in silence. As soon as she got in she told Sam to get ready for bed, to which he replied he wasn't tired. One look and he decided that it wasn't worth an argument. She heard him head upstairs and close his door before she went into the living room and headed for the liquor cabinet. She just needed a little something, just one glass to take the edge off. She pulled out a bottle of bourbon and a glass. She was in the middle of unscrewing the top when her mind returned to her conversation with Darryl that afternoon. The memory of bottles clinking together, his demeanor, the argument in the kitchen, and the door slamming shut. Why? Why didn't she just take him in? She placed the bottle down and screwed the top back on without pouring a drink. This wasn't the way. Ben was right. At some point she had to face all the problems she was dealing with and not hide behind drink or anything that would dull her senses. Skylar headed over to the recliner chair in the corner of the room and slumped into it.

* * *

The next morning she awoke to Sam shaking her. "Come on, I'm going to be late for school."

She blinked hard. Her mouth was dry as she sat up and took in the world around her. She'd fallen asleep in her clothes, in the same chair from the night before. "What time is it?"

He pointed to the clock.

"Oh man. Okay, have you had breakfast?"

"Yep."

"What about lunch? Have you made it?"

"Already on top of it. Let's just get in the truck."

She nodded, scooped up her keys and headed out to take him to school. When they pulled up outside and Sam got out, Skylar called out to him. "Remember. If you have any trouble call me. Let's not see a repeat of yesterday."

"It won't happen."

She smiled. "Okay. Have a good day."

* * *

After taking a shower and making her way to the police department, she took a deep breath preparing herself for the onslaught from Davenport, Harvey and probably all of the staff. Sure enough as she walked through the doors she got several looks of disappointment. Thankfully it didn't look like Davenport and Harvey were in yet. She moved quickly to her desk and got started pulling up the case file on Nick. Skylar did a search on Rapid Loans to see what she could find online. It wasn't uncommon to see people leaving reviews of establishments and with the Outlaws funding the operation there had to be several accusations being thrown at them.

Strangely, there were none. Just glowing reviews. It didn't add up. Not everyone would have been able to pay their loan back, which meant getting a call from either Bo or worse — the Outlaws. If that was the case there would have been a long list of people who had wound up in the hospital or gone missing in Miami. There was none. Perhaps no one spoke up out of fear.

"Well here she is, the lady of the house," Hanson said coming up behind her all stealth like and perching on the corner of her desk. He had a coffee in hand and a smug grin on his face. "Reid, rumor has it you screwed up big time. I hear you might not make it out of this one with your badge intact. Do you have anything to say?" He pretended his pastry that morning was a microphone by jabbing it in her face. Skylar scowled at him and tried to remain focused on her search. Hanson turned his head towards the computer.

"Oh it's closed. Out of business," he said.

"Yeah, I knew that."

"And you're on the wrong website. Shouldn't you be browsing job sites?"

"Hilarious."

He groaned and stifled a laugh. "Got some good news for you though. We managed to find Darryl last night. Yep, guy was hanging out down at Ruby's Bar. Can you imagine that? Of all the places to go and stay low, he chooses the one which is currently under surveillance."

Skylar's ears perked up. "Where is he?"

"In the cells sleeping off one hell of a hangover probably."

She got up and headed for the stairs that led down to the cells.

"Um you might want to get permission from Davenport before—"

She was already halfway down the staircase when he said that. Had it been last night she might have ripped off a few of his limbs but she'd had the evening to process it and let go of all the negative emotion towards him. As she rounded the corner that led past six cells, she looked through the slim glass window on each of the thick steel doors. Only three of them were occupied. The second had Darryl in it. He was lying on his side in a fetal position. Skylar inserted the key and pulled the door open. She glanced up at the camera outside before entering. All the cells were being monitored so she couldn't exactly lash out and of course if she did she would be facing a civil lawsuit, however, that didn't mean she couldn't shake him up a bit.

"Wake up!"

He stirred, groaned and rolled over looking at her

before blinking.

"Am I getting out?"

"Not for a long time. I'm going to make sure that you spend a good amount of time behind bars."

"Whatever, screw you."

As he rolled over she noticed his shirt pull down ever so slightly to reveal a small tattoo on his neck. She crouched over him and pulled back the shirt remembering what the bartender said about a man having a dragon tattoo. Sure enough, there it was. She hadn't seen it when he came in the door yesterday as it was on the opposite side of his neck and hidden by his jacket collar.

"You with the Outlaws?"

He snorted. "Was."

"Two nights ago, were you at Ruby's Bar?"

"What if I was?"

"Listen, I've not had a coffee today. In fact, I'm trying to quit the damn stuff because I'm tired of the drama between two cafés here in town but that's neither here nor there. My point is. I have little patience for assholes who lie, and even less for those who beat up a woman. Now get up!"

She seized him by the scruff of his neck and pulled him up.

"Hey. Hey!" he said. "All right."

Once she had him sitting upright Skylar leaned against the wall on the far side of the cell and began her questioning.

"Were you at Ruby's or not?"

"I might have been. What's it worth to me?"

"It's worth not being charged with a murder."

"A murder? I haven't murdered anyone."

"Were you there?"

"Yeah. I was there. I met up with an old friend of mine."

"A biker?"

He sighed and stared down at his knuckles which were bruised. The thought of Jenna's bruised and cut face flashed across her mind. It took everything she had not to reach across and beat the living daylights out of him.

"Look, it's no mystery me and Jenna have been having problems."

"Problems? Is that what you call it? You know, I have problems but I don't resort to beating the crap out of women. Men? Um, I'm thinking about that today."

His eyes widened. Yeah, he got the point.

"I used to run with the Outlaws until I met Jenna." He looked down despondently. "She made me see a life outside of it all. Away from the violence."

"Away from the violence?" She snorted, the irony wasn't wasted.

"Look, you know what, I get it. You think I'm a monster and you're right. I need help." He shook his head as if he didn't know what to say. "Believe me or not but I love Jenna."

"You call beating her to a pulp love?" He glanced up but didn't reply. "So?"

"I was there, we had a few drinks and left later that evening."

"You mean you were thrown out."

"Thrown out, left, it's all the same."

"Did you have a run-in with someone by the name of Nick Hammond?"

"Who?"

"Barrel-chested man, lawyer, was paying for drinks and groping women."

"Oh, him." He chuckled. "Yeah, he came on to my buddy's gal. So he slapped him a few times and the bouncers threw us out."

"Where did you go after that?"

"Why?"

"Where?"

He blew out his cheeks. "I headed to another bar. Harry's. After that I was dropped off home around eleven."

"And your buddy?"

"He went back to Miami."

"Has your buddy got a name?"

"Bo Gonzales."

seat.

"Well we have him now," he said. "What have you managed to dig up so far on the Nick Hammond situation?"

"We're still waiting back on the ME for results but I should have those today," Harvey said.

"And you, Skylar?" Davenport asked.

She scratched her neck. "Yeah, we've made some progress. It seems our boy down there in the cell, Darryl, he used to run with the Outlaws and on the night Nick died, he was the one down at the bar."

Harvey turned in his seat with a look of astonishment. "Are you sure?"

"I got a confession out of him. And get this… the guy that was with him that night was Bo Gonzales."

"Rapid Loans owner. Hold on a minute. But wasn't Keith there on the same night?"

"Bingo. And all three don't have alibis. Bo and Darryl were kicked out. According to the bartender, Keith left before that."

All three of them sat there staring at one another chewing it over.

"Then it's possible that any one of them could have could have done it."

"Exactly," Skylar said.

Davenport took a sip of his coffee. "Do we have the video?"

Skylar frowned. "What?"

"The video that was used for blackmail. Do we have that as evidence in all of this? I mean we assume that this is what is behind all of this, right?"

"I'll look into that," Harvey said. "The next step is to find this Bo Gonzales."

Skylar reached into her jacket and pulled out her notepad. "Already one step ahead. Darryl gave us the address for his friend in Miami. You ready to catch a flight?"

Harvey's eyes widened. "Today?"

"Yeah."

"But you have Sam to look after."

It suddenly dawned on her. "Oh man."

"Now you know what family life is like," Harvey said with a smile on his face.

"Harvey, take Hanson with you," Davenport said leaning forward across his desk.

"What? But captain..." Harvey protested. "We can just call the Miami-Dade Police Department and have them swing by the address."

"I want you to be there. I've seen these things go south all the time."

He groaned.

"Seriously, Harvey. You have the best job in the world. Who gets to fly to Miami and do these kinds of things?" Davenport said.

"Well can I leave Hanson here?"

"No. I don't want this screwed up."

"And by that you mean?"

"Look, just take him with you."

Harvey blew out his cheeks and looked over at Skylar. Skylar had a smirk on her face. She knew Harvey hated

Hanson. The animosity between them was palpable at the best of times. Harvey still blamed Hanson for raiding Callum Jackson's place when he knew his sister was in danger. The reality was there were other women involved and many of them were saved because of Hanson's quick decision. The fact was he was bitter over his sister's death and until Callum was behind bars he was looking for anyone to punish.

"And what about me, captain?" Skylar asked.

"Get me the report from the ME's office and get back in with Keith White and apply a bit more pressure. Perhaps he's still holding back."

She nodded and got up and opened the door. Harvey brushed past her. He was in a foul mood. He crossed the office and pointed to Hanson. "You. Let's go. We have a flight to catch."

Hanson scooped up his jacket from the back of his chair, tossed a half-eaten apple into the trash and tried to catch up. Harvey pushed out of the office and was gone in less than sixty seconds. There was something about the way he was acting that felt off. Sure, Skylar got on his nerves at times, and of course she wasn't perfect or the easiest to work with, but he just seemed off-kilter. Although she was liable to heap more hot coals on her head, Skylar scooped up a phone and plunked herself down at her desk to make a call to Elizabeth. She was working at her antiques business in town. It was a nice little store that sold all manner of unique items from all over the South. Skylar had been in and bought a few items for the boat.

"Baker's Antiques."

"Elizabeth, it's Skylar."

"Oh hi hon, how are yah?"

"Good. I was just hoping to talk to you about Harvey."

"Oh no," she groaned. "What's he done now?"

She leaned back in her chair and put her feet up on the corner of her table. "Is there anything I should know? Is he going through some kind of manopause?"

"Manopause?" She laughed. "I like that." Elizabeth

took a deep breath. "He's cranky, right?"

"Is he ever. He raked me over the coals about the way things went with Jenna."

"Oh that." Her tone of voice went soft. "Yeah. I heard about it last night. Terrible."

"I did everything I could."

"I'm sure you did, Skylar. You have to understand something about Harvey. But before I tell you, promise me you won't say anything."

"You have my word."

"I mean it."

"My lips are sealed."

There was a pause as she hesitated. "His mother was a victim of domestic abuse. It was a long time ago and she survived but she nearly died from it."

Skylar felt her stomach twist.

"He was there the night it happened. He froze. Didn't know what to do."

"I didn't know."

"Yeah, so if he rides you hard over it, that's why. I

thought it was best you knew being as you work with him and all."

"Anything else?"

"Why don't you come for dinner more often?"

"I don't want to intrude and with the foul mood Harvey has been in lately I just thought it was best I stayed out of the way."

She chuckled. "Believe me, I have days when I don't want to be around him as well."

They chatted for a while before Skylar had to go. After getting off the phone she felt a little bit more relieved than before. There was still so much to Harvey that she was just learning about. He was like an onion. Behind every new layer of skin was something new. He had his wounds, his baggage, his issues but he just did a better job of covering them up.

* * *

About two and a half hours later, Harvey and Hanson touched down in Miami. It was sweltering hot, and overcrowded.

"You know, Baker, you really should work on your conversational skills."

"And you should work on giving your mouth a break," he said as they headed out to collect their rental car.

"All this animosity towards me can't be good for your ulcer."

"Ulcer?"

"Yeah, an old-timer like you should have a dozen of them by now."

"I'll have you know…"

"Oh, this looks like our ride," Hanson said cutting him off and heading over to a blue Ford SUV. He popped the trunk and tossed in a bag.

"I don't know why you insisted on picking up clothes. We are only going to be here until this evening."

"You never can be too careful," Hanson said. "This one time…"

"Save it," Harvey said cutting him off. He knew if he got him started he would just end up yakking for the next half an hour. He glanced at his watch as he got into the driver's side and waited for Hanson. They had a meeting with a lieutenant of the Miami-Dade Police Department just off Miami Gardens just to make sure they were in the loop. It had been a long while since he'd been down here. The last time he'd visited Miami was seven years ago when he and his wife took a cruise to the Bahamas. Since then he really hadn't had a vacation so to speak. Sure, he'd had a few days here and there but that wasn't time off. He needed a mental break from it all.

On the way over, Hanson continued to go on like a broken record about all manner of stuff, much of which had no bearing on the case. All Harvey wanted to do was collect Bo and get the hell back to Carrabelle. He'd arranged to take in a ball game with his kid later that evening but at the rate things were going it wouldn't be happening.

"Anyway, so I go and see this acupuncture guy for stress. I'm telling you, Baker, it does wonders. You really should go and check it out. I know it sounds like mumbo jumbo but these Chinese folks really know what they are doing. He was telling me I had to work with my Chi energy and breathe more. He said…"

"Did he say you talk too much?" Harvey muttered.

"Who stuck something up your rear end?"

"Look, I just want to get back."

"Ah the missus riding you again? Has she got one of those honey-do lists? That's why I never got married. It's too much work. You know, when I go home I like to chill and relax. I don't want a million jobs around the house."

"Hanson!"

"Okay. Okay. Geesh."

There was a long pause as both of them looked out the windows at the traffic clogging up the roads. Harvey hated the big cities. Too much traffic. Too much smog. Too many people. It made his skin crawl. At one time Elizabeth had wanted to move to Tallahassee because she thought owning an antiques store there would be more profitable but Harvey nipped that idea in the bud immediately.

"Tell me something, Hanson. Does Davenport ever

talk to you about me?"

He chuckled. "Paranoid, are we?"

"Curious."

"Occasionally," he said pulling out a bottle of water from a bag around his shoulder and cracking the top. "A couple of days ago he wanted me to handle a few files."

"The Summers and Thompson cases?" Harvey asked.

"Yeah."

Harvey rolled his eyes and sighed. "Great."

"Ah he does that. Don't worry, he goes through phases where he will hand off a case to one officer then take it away and give it to another. I swear it's some kind of OCD. He did it to me in March and April with the…"

"Parkinson and Ellis cases?"

He laughed. "Ah so you ended up with them."

"Yeah," Harvey said.

"I swear Davenport needs his head checked."

Harvey laughed as they pulled up outside the cream-colored building at 18805 27th Avenue. It had been a long time since he'd spent any time working alongside

Hanson. Before Harvey lost his sister they got along well. So much had changed since then. They parked and headed into the building. Outside the temperature was extraordinarily high. It was too hot to be out and he didn't like the idea of camping outside Bo Gonzales' home. The Miami-Dade Police Department said they would send over a few plainclothes officers to check out his apartment while they were making their way down, on the off chance they spotted him.

"Detective. Good to see you."

"Please tell me you found him?" Harvey said, hoping the trip could be cut short.

"Unfortunately no. They've been outside his place all day. No one has come or gone. Though I do have some good news for you. We managed to pull in one of the Outlaws and he has an interesting story to tell about that night. Seems he was involved in bringing funds to Rapid Loans. If you want to come this way I'll take you to him."

Chapter 11

Skylar looked at the body of Nick Hammond. He was laid out on one of the sterile workbenches inside the medical examiner's office. She was there to get the update and to check that there wasn't anything they'd overlooked. A guy in his early twenties, thin frame, wearing specs and fumbling around with paperwork, hurried over.

He pushed up his specs that had slipped down his nose and squinted.

"The name's Jameson, and you are?"

"Skylar Reid," she replied without taking her eyes off Nick. His body was covered with a white sheet up to his chest. His skin was pale and there was excessive bruising around the chest area.

"Any word on Jenna?" Jameson asked.

"She's stable."

He shook his head. "I kind of feel lost without her

here. She really was my lifeline," Jameson said, dropping his pen. Skylar cut him a glance, noticing how anxious he was acting.

"So what have you got for me?"

"Well our initial findings led us to believe that the victim had died from blunt force trauma to the chest area, which you can see here," he said pointing to his chest, which was a deep shade of purple. "Now while the crash played a role and may have led to a heart attack, it actually wasn't that which killed him. With Jenna gone, and with the urgency of the case, I had them put a rush on the lab results and it appears our victim didn't die from the heart attack. It was actually from poisoning."

"Poisoning?"

"His body had a large amount of ethylene glycol. Which means he was poisoned by antifreeze."

"But wouldn't he have tasted that?"

"Not if it was mixed inside another drink. It has a sweet taste."

"Or if he'd already had one too many drinks," Skylar

said.

"That as well," Jameson said.

Skylar tapped him on the shoulder. "There is hope for you yet, young padawan."

* * *

After exiting the medical examiner's office, Skylar was making her way back to her truck when her phone began buzzing in her pocket. She fished it out and checked the caller ID. It was the school.

"Hello?"

"Ms. Reid, there has been an incident. Can you come to the school and pick up Sam?"

"Oh please tell me he has not been beaten up. I don't think I can…"

"No. Sam is fine. It's what he did to one of the kids."

Skylar's stomach sank. She quickly hung up and hopped into her vehicle. Within five minutes she was parked outside the school and double-timed it down the hallway towards the reception area. This time she didn't have to wait long. Principal Myers was already there to greet her along with Sam who was sitting outside her office. The moment he saw her his face lit up but Skylar just frowned and walked past him into Myers' office.

Once the door was closed and she'd taken a seat, Myers clasped her hands together, pursed her lips and breathed in deeply as if she was readying a speech she had been looking forward to giving for a long time.

"It appears Sam got into an argument with one of the boys here at the school this morning and instead of dealing with it by coming to one of the teachers he decided to take matters into his own hands. Now a student has two black eyes, and a cut lip."

"This student wouldn't by any chance be the same one that has been picking on him for the last two weeks, would it?"

"Ms. Reid. I think you are missing the point here. This kind of behavior will not be tolerated. We have a zero tolerance for bullying."

"How do you know it wasn't self-defense?"

"Whether it was self-defense or not doesn't matter. I

can't have students going home with black eyes and cut lips."

"Of course not except when it's Sam."

"I'm not sure what you are implying," Myers said.

"He's been bullied for over two weeks and no one has done anything."

"He should have come to us."

"I think a bruised eye should have been cause for concern, Ms. Myers. I thought your teachers are meant to look out for this kind of stuff?"

"They do if the student shows up for school."

"Then maybe you can explain why Sam came home with a bruised eye?"

"I understand you are frustrated but this conversation is about what Sam has done to another student. I cannot speak for what did or did not occur several days ago."

"I think it has a huge bearing on this situation. If you push people enough, eventually they are going to push back. That's what's happened here. This sounds like nothing more than self-defense."

"That's not what other students have said. They said that Sam was the aggressor."

Skylar got up. "Do you mind?" she said opening the door. "I'm gathering you have asked Sam what happened, yes?"

"Ms. Reid."

Skylar stepped out. "Sam, you care to join us so we can discuss what happened here?"

He got up and walked in as Myers protested. "Ms. Reid. This is not how we deal with matters."

"No? Well maybe that's the problem," Skylar said. Both she and Sam took a seat and Myers pouted for a second or two and then when she realized she wasn't going to get her way, she made a gesture with her hand towards Sam.

"Sam, you want to explain what happened?" Skylar asked.

He looked reluctant at first but slowly he began to retell what occurred. "I was on my way out for break when Kirk Bowman and his goons pulled me into one of the bathrooms and tried to flush my head down the toilet. I told them to back off and pushed back but they wouldn't listen. They just kept dragging me towards the toilet so I punched Kirk in the nuts, kicked his buddy in the knee and then managed to get up. I tried to get out the door but Steve, Kirk's other friend, grabbed me. I used that move you showed me. You know the one where you use their weight against them. Anyway I threw him into the door behind me. Of course that blocked my way and by then Kirk was back up and coming at me. I used that block and punch technique and..."

As he continued to go on, Skylar could see the look of horror on Ms. Myers' face as Sam relayed all the techniques she'd taught him.

"... Anyway, that's what happened."

"Okay, Sam. If you want to head back out, I'll finish up here," Skylar said.

The second the door was closed Myers tore into Skylar. "Are you in the habit of teaching your son how to hurt others? I cannot believe that."

"Hold on a minute. First, he's not my son. Which only goes to show you don't pay attention to details. Second, I did not teach him how to hurt others. I taught him how to protect himself. There is a big difference. And, for your information, if the teachers here aren't going to watch out for him, what do you expect him to do? Take a beating? Because believe me, Ms. Myers, this situation could have very well ended with Sam being the one with two black eyes and a cut lip. Then what would you have done?"

"I would be speaking with the other boys' parents."

"Really? Because as far as I know in the two weeks that they've been pounding on him, your school hasn't done squat!"

Myers leaned over her table. "You know, I've heard about you. The new cop in town causing all manner of trouble. Let me tell you something…"

Skylar got up and leaned across the table. "No, let me stop you right here. If you want to take this any further by all means — go ahead but I'm pretty sure people will be very interested in knowing how this school deals with bullying."

"But…"

"I think we are done here. It was self-defense."

Skylar headed towards the door and stepped outside. "Sam. I will be here to pick you up at the end of the day. Enjoy your day."

He got this smile on his face as she walked away.

* * *

Harvey walked out of the interview room shaking his head. The conversation with the member of the Outlaws was a complete letdown. The only information he had was to confirm that the Outlaws were the funding source behind Rapid Loans and that Bo Gonzales had a hit on his head for failing to pay them back. The Outlaws believed he concocted the whole story of his database being wiped in order to take the money they'd given him for clients and now he was keeping it for himself.

"Makes you wonder why he would have agreed to get in bed with the Outlaws in the first place," Hanson said.

"Don't these people ever think about the long-term problems that could arise?"

"These kinds of people don't think, period," Harvey said as they headed out of the department and made their way back to the rental. "I knew this was a bad idea from the beginning. Contacting Miami has only screwed this up. Chances are Miami's plainclothes guys have been spotted by him and now he won't come within a mile of that address."

"Here's the bit I don't get. If this Darryl guy was running with the Outlaws and he had the address of Bo. Surely the Outlaws have already checked that address?"

"That was the reason I was griping about coming all the way here. I think it's a wild goose chase. Chances of him being in Miami are slim to none. These bikers don't play around. We are talking about an excessive amount of money that he owes them. Let's say he has a hundred clients and each of them need a loan for ten grand. That's a whole lot of money to be on the hook for."

"Yes and no," Hanson said. "It's obviously a means of

laundering drug money by running through a legit company. Rapid Loans earns back the money plus interest, which I might add is probably an excessive amount of interest — and both parties are happy. They get their cash back plus some extra on top."

Harvey chewed it over as they made their way through the endless bumper-to-bumper traffic and arrived at the address of one Bo Gonzales. They had the license plate number of the officers that were watching the place, and when they arrived Harvey approached them, sliding up the side of the vehicle and scaring the living daylights out of them by banging on the window.

The window dropped.

"Here to take over."

"From Carrabelle?"

"That would be us. You seen anything?"

"Not even a mailman," the officer replied.

They thanked them and watched them drive away before Hanson was about to park the SUV in the same spot.

"Don't park there," Harvey said.

"Why not?"

"Hanson. Think. If Bo did kill our man, and he's been keeping tabs on this place, he will be looking for anyone that is either a cop or biker. And if he already spotted Miami's guys, it's not going to help us parking in the same spot, now is it?"

"You have a point. So where do you want to go?"

"Well I'm not waiting here for him to show. We are going to visit his ex-wife. If anyone would know where he is, she would." Harvey began tapping into the GPS the address he'd managed to get from Axl who had Nick Hammond's notebook. "It's not far from here. Hang a left down here and it will guide you the rest of the way."

"Yes sir," Hanson said in a sarcastic manner.

Ms. Wendy Gonzales lived in a luxury condo that overlooked South Beach. After having taken her husband for every penny he had and destroying his livelihood, she hadn't wasted any time in setting herself up in a crib with the best view in Florida, and one that had high-end security. After spending close to twenty minutes trying to find a parking spot, and another twenty hiking through the sweltering heat, they made it to her forty-five-story condo. The place must have just been built as there wasn't a speck of dust in it, and the floors, doors, and front desk were gleaming. It even had that new smell in the air.

"Can I help you?" a front desk clerk asked.

"We're here to see a Ms. Gonzales."

"Is she expecting you?"

"Yes, I was speaking with her by phone. The name is Harvey Baker. We're from the police department." He pulled out his badge.

He hadn't called her but he thought if he said that Wendy might assume she'd spoken with him and let him up. It was an old trick that worked in the past. People were curious by nature and he used it to his advantage.

The front desk clerk turned and placed a phone call. A couple of seconds later he motioned with his head towards the elevator. "She's on floor forty-one. Number

122."

Harvey thanked him and headed over to the elevators. There was a cleaner dusting the gold buttons. Hanson made a comment that once the cleaner was done she could do his apartment in Carrabelle if she wanted. He offered to pay her $20. The woman rolled her eyes and walked away as they stepped into the lift.

When they arrived outside her apartment the door was already open.

"Come in, gentlemen," a female voice said from inside. The inside of the condo was amazing. It was a three-bedroom residence with a den, floor-to-ceiling windows, sliding glass doors in the main living area, a private terrace with a glassed-in balcony and marble counters. No expense had been spared. They were greeted by a good-looking woman in her late thirties. She had long dark hair that flowed down her back and was so smooth and straight it almost looked fake. She was wearing a yoga outfit and was in the middle of doing downward dog. Her rear end was facing them as they spotted her. Hanson nudged Harvey in the ribs as they both took in the sight of her shapely butt.

"Ms. Gonzales."

"Ugh. I'm divorced from that pig. It's now Wendy Owen. Please call me Wendy."

"Wendy. We were hoping you might be able to shed some light on where your ex-husband is."

She straightened up breathing heavily and walked over to a table to scoop up a bottle of water. "Why, what's he done now?"

"It's not exactly what he's done as it is what he might have done."

"Which is?"

"Nick Hammond is dead, Wendy," Harvey said.

She stopped drinking and looked down at the floor shaking her head.

"Are you okay?" Hanson asked stepping forward to brace her.

"Yeah, I just need a second." Hanson guided her to a seat and the color in her face came back. "Nick was real good to me. Had it not been for him I would have still been with that man and penniless. What happened?"

"As far as we know right now he was forced off the road, and had a heart attack. We are still waiting to hear back from the medical examiner. In fact they probably have the results by now."

"He got to him, didn't he?

Harvey frowned. "He?"

Chapter 12

It seemed that Wendy knew more about Keith than what had been revealed to the police. "The guy was a lunatic, showing up at our business at all hours wanting more money."

"More money? But I thought he had problems paying back his loans."

"Keith? No. He paid on time like clockwork. There wasn't one payment he missed. Problem wasn't with what he owed, it was with me. He wanted to take me out. I wouldn't let him. It was just creepy. I told Bo but he wouldn't do anything about it because," she made quote signs with her fingers, "he is a client and a good one." She shook her head and took another sip of her drink. "Bo just thought I was seeking attention or interrupting his meetings with important new clients. Well we all know who those new clients were. He was cheating on me. Anyway, Keith showed up here one night all drunk and

Bo wasn't around. He tried forcing himself on me and I had to get physical."

"Physical?"

"I slapped him and kneed him in the privates. Then, I went and got the .45 from the back office and told him if he ever came around again I would kill him."

Harvey raised his eyebrow and she noticed. "Of course I wouldn't kill him but I had to say that to get him out of here. The guy was like a fly in the ointment, he just wouldn't go away. Now you would think this would stop him, well it didn't. He ended up stalking me, sending me flowers and gifts and apologizing profusely and confessing his undying love for me. It was beyond sickening."

"Why didn't you go to the cops?"

"Bo had a no-cop policy. Can you imagine them showing up here asking questions? They would want to know what he did for a living, and if they turned their attention on Keith who knows what he would have said."

"About?"

"About our business."

"So he knew about the Outlaws funding it all."

She was hesitant to respond to that.

"It's okay, we already know. I'm not gonna bust you over being involved in an illegal operation that no longer exists. We are trying to get to the bottom of this murder."

She nodded. "Not at first." She walked across the room and collected a vape pen and began sucking on it before blowing a cloud of smoke. "Detective, most of the people that walked through our doors just wanted cash until their next payday. We did a lot of payday loans. Beyond that it was folks with bad credit. Those who were turned down by banks. It was easy for us to approve them as we always had the Outlaws ready at our beck and call. In many ways it was the perfect kind of operation to run." She took another hit on her vape pen. "Anyway, Keith was a different kettle of fish. He went through money like water. He always paid back until the last time. He'd withdrawn a huge amount of money from us. I wasn't even involved in the transaction, I just know from Bo that it was a lot. Far more than he'd ever done. Usually Keith would want a couple of thousand, twenty thousand tops. But this was up somewhere in the six-figure range. That's all Bo told me." She walked over to the window and Harvey studied her. "Bo was gloating about how much interest he was going to make off this deal." She took a deep breath. "Anyway, I told him it wasn't a good idea to lend out that much but he trusted Keith. We had already been through like sixty or more transactions. He was one of our best clients, you could say. Now I think he was preparing us. You know, trying to gain our trust."

Hanson was listening but at the same time admiring some of the sculptures in her condo. At one point he accidentally nudged one and it toppled. He caught it at the last second and thankfully Wendy wasn't looking but it was close. Harvey scowled at him and Hanson tossed his hands up like a kid that had been caught with his fingers in the cookie jar.

"Go on," Harvey said.

"So the day of payment rolls around and Keith doesn't show up. At first Bo doesn't sweat it. He thinks he'll get a call the next day. Next day — no call. No show. No money. Bo phoned him and left countless messages and then by the third day he flew out to Carrabelle to find him."

"And did he?"

"No. He was in a state when he got back. Cursing, smashing up furniture and then he started to panic. You see, the way it worked was depending on the loan arrangement, if they had a couple of years to pay it back, we would get a visit once a month from Brent Rutz, one of the guys in the Outlaws. He would make sure that everything was flowing nicely, clients were paying back, discuss any late payers and leave us with more money for new clients. Well, in all previous loans, Keith had said he would pay back within a month. He'd become such a good client that even the Outlaws knew about him. It was like a running joke down here that he was probably using the money down at the casinos and had some gig on the side that made sure he made back his money. That's the only way we could think he was able to come up with the money again so fast. I swear it was uncanny. What you need to understand is nearly all of the people who come to us for loans pay back but there is a fraction that don't. In which case the Outlaws step in and handle it. Sometimes that is all it takes to get that person back in here the following month with money, sometimes..." She trailed off and Harvey picked up on hesitation to continue.

"They killed them?"

She shrugged. "I don't know. All I know is that I didn't feel safe in that environment. It was toxic. If it wasn't the Outlaws flying off the handle when they learned about someone who had missed several payments it was Bo. He was literally riding the razor's edge. I knew one of these days it would go wrong and they would come after him."

Harvey threw up a hand. "Okay, I understand what you are trying to get at here but it was Nick Hammond that was murdered, not your ex-husband. Now Keith told us that he had fallen behind on payments and that he recorded your husband in the arms of another woman. Why didn't he just give you the tape?"

"I don't know, maybe because he thought he could trust Nick. Maybe he wanted to store it in a safe place just in case Bo came knocking? Maybe he knew that Nick needed the money. How would I know?"

"A lawyer that needs money?" Hanson chuckled

"He makes a good point. Why would Nick need money?" Harvey added.

"Look, I don't know. All I know is that after he handed that video over and Nick got me out of this situation, he and I were intimate."

"You and Nick got together?"

"Nick was a good man with a shitty wife and even worse friends. You have to understand, detectives, if it wasn't for Nick I would either still be in that relationship or dead. Once I saw that video, and Nick promised me he could help me win a nice settlement, I knew I would have the means to walk away and start a new life."

"But not before you wiped his database."

"My ex-husband is an idiot. Oh he knew how to talk his way into the big game but he had no idea when it came to finances, paying taxes, doing books. He left all that to me. I knew exactly what to do to screw him over."

"But by wiping that database you must have known that the Outlaws would come for you."

"That's why I live here. It's safe and I only let up…"

"Cops you haven't met?" Hanson said. She stared back and realized the error of her ways. For all her smart talk, she wasn't exactly smart. She narrowed her eyes at Hanson and continued trying to explain.

"I've seen how the Outlaws operate. They stay clear of places like this. Anywhere there is security, cameras. It's not their way. If they are going to take someone out they will wait until they leave the building."

"So aren't you afraid of that?" Harvey asked.

"They don't even know I'm here."

"We found you. Your name, address and phone number were listed among Nick's client files."

She shrugged and laughed. "But you're the police. It's

your job to sniff around. No, the way the Outlaws view it, it's Bo who is responsible for the loss of their money, not some brain-dead ex-wife."

"Brain-dead?"

"It was one of the many names he called me in front of them."

Hanson put down a glass skull on the table that he was admiring. "I can see why you left him."

She puffed away on her vape pen looking even more stressed out. "Anyway, if anyone wanted to kill him it would have been Keith. He's a lunatic. He flew off the handle once he found out that Nick had handed over his only bargaining chip. That's who you need to be talking to, not Bo."

"But do you know where Bo is staying?"

"I can phone around. I'm sure it wouldn't be hard to find him."

"If it's not hard for you," Hanson asked, "then why haven't the Outlaws found him?"

"As stupid as my ex-husband was, he knew to keep

business and his personal life separate. He was very careful. He never followed the same route into work on a given day, he never left at the same time and he had multiple ways to avoid detection."

"Sounds like Jason Bourne," Hanson said, chuckling to himself.

Wendy scowled. "It's called insurance when you're dealing with a biker gang who can end you faster than a New York minute."

Harvey nodded. It made sense. "Well while you do that I'm going to step outside and have a word with my partner." Harvey gave a nod to Hanson and he walked away from a huge fish tank and joined him outside in the corridor.

"So, we're partners?" Hanson smiled.

"Figure of speech," Harvey said, quickly correcting him. "Look, once we have that address we'll go pay him a visit. I'm gonna make a quick call to Reid and get her to have another word with Keith."

They walked down the hallway a little to a vending

machine area and Hanson slotted some money into the machine to get out a can of Coke.

"You know that stuff is going to rot a hole in your stomach."

"It tastes good, we don't live long," Hanson said.

Harvey pulled his phone out. "You'll live longer if you don't drink that. Have you seen what that can do to a coin? It's acid in a can."

He cracked it open while Harvey made the call. He stood by the doorway watching Hanson struggle to get a pack of chips to drop. It happened all the time to him at the department. Why the vending companies couldn't come up with better technology was beyond him.

"Ah, good, Reid. Finally you pick up."

"Finally?" Skylar replied.

"Well you do tend to ignore it."

"What do you need?"

"Keith White. Is he still being held?"

"As far as I know. They consider him a flight risk but without anything to hold him he might be let out today,"

Skylar replied.

"Well, we might have the smoking gun in the way of Bo's wife."

"I thought you were there for him."

"We haven't found him yet. I did a little digging around and thought she would know."

"Right. When in doubt. Ask the wife."

"Exactly. Anyway, here's what you need to know."

Harvey updated her on the conversation with Wendy. When he was done he glanced down the hallway and saw the stairwell door open. Two hulking guys wearing suits came out, both of them were holding briefcases. They looked like Mormons, angry ones. He looked away.

"So you think you can do that?" Harvey asked.

"Oh come on!" Hanson said kicking the vending machine.

"Yeah. Leave it with me. I'll fit it in between my arguments with the school and dealing with Darryl," Skylar said.

"Arguments with the school? You know what, don't

tell me, I don't want to know."

Right then they heard gunshots. Harvey looked down the hall and saw the two men emerge from Wendy's condo. They cut him a glance, and he reached for his service weapon. Everything seemed to slow in those seconds as they opened fire and made a dash for the stairwell.

Harvey pulled back crashing into Hanson to escape the rounds peppering the walls.

The onslaught of gunfire didn't last long. Harvey sneaked a peek around the corner and the guys were gone. He darted out heading for Wendy's condo keeping his gun trained on the stairwell door.

The moment he stepped through the door he knew it was bad.

The floor was covered in blood, and lying motionless was Wendy.

"Hanson, call the cops and an ambulance, now."

He rushed out after the men, slipping into the stairwell. He heard the sound of a door closing farther down. Harvey hurried down holding his weapon and taking multiple steps at a time. He landed hard and his shoulder smashed into the wall. When he was down on the fifth floor several residents came out and screamed at the sight of his gun.

"It's okay, I'm a cop," he said pressing on hoping to catch up with them before they escaped. Before he'd even reached the ground floor he heard more gunfire. He hurried, trying not to trip on the way down. When he made it to the lobby, he saw a security guard on the ground. He wasn't dead but he was gripping his shoulder and his gun was across the floor. The front desk clerk jabbed his finger in the direction of where they had gone as Harvey raced after them.

He was close to the revolving doors when more gunfire ensued, this time glass shattered and he hit the ground.

"Get down," he shouted to a woman and her young child. Glass scattered across the granite floors. He heard the squeal of tires and then it was over. Harvey darted out into the busy street but the vehicle was already gone.

Chapter 13

Skylar was on her way to speak to Keith when Reznik phoned her with an update on the surveillance footage he'd managed to obtain. She swerved off to the edge of the road to take the call. "I hope this is good as I'm a little busy."

"Even though the footage inside the bar wasn't good, I did manage to obtain footage from a restaurant across the street. Now while I didn't see anyone following Nick when he left that evening, I did see someone who said they weren't there that night," Resnik said.

"Who?"

"You ready for this?"

"Reznik, just spit it out."

"Mrs. Hammond."

"What was she doing?"

"Who knows? She's seen entering the establishment an hour after Nick arrived and then she leaves before him. I swear I had a hard time getting this footage."

"The restaurant wouldn't hand it over?"

"No, they were more than willing to help but they had misplaced the backup they had and well, if we didn't have this there would be no way of knowing she was there. By the way, I spoke to the owner. I told him he needed to upgrade his equipment and get the cameras placed in better spots as it wasn't just so they could record any trouble but so they could protect themselves. That small ass camera they had behind the bar is a joke. What's that meant to record? The bartenders' asses?"

"You would go there," Skylar said.

He chuckled.

"Okay, thanks Reznik."

"I hear Harvey is in Miami."

"Gotta go," Skylar said, quickly hanging up. She knew if she didn't get off then he would keep yakking for the next half an hour. Instead of heading to see Keith she decided to swing by the Hammond residence and find out why she'd lied about where she was that night. There were few things that frustrated her in a murder case, but lying was one of them. She didn't like to be played and yet at the same time she knew it came with the territory. Criminals were masters at it, at least those who had something to hide. As she drove over to Bay Avenue she ran through some of the reasons why Nancy might have wanted Nick dead. There was the obvious, his cheating, and then there were financial reasons, he was blowing through her money. She'd certainly seen people murdered for less.

She was crossing through the main stretch of town when her truck started making funky noises. "Come on, baby. Not now." She gave the dashboard a pat thinking that might have some bearing on whether or not it would screw her over today or give her another twenty-four hours. She'd considered buying another vehicle and gone out of her way to visit a few dealerships but the process was a nightmare. It infuriated her to no end. The worst one had advertised over forty different vehicles of a certain make and model but when she turned up at the showroom there were only five. When she asked why they were still advertising these models, they said they hadn't got around to updating their website. Yeah, a likely story. So she asked to test drive one and they told her she was going to have to drive it around the lot because they didn't have a plate for it. She couldn't believe it. What dealership required a person to drive a car around the lot to determine if they wanted to buy it? It was around that point that she pulled out her badge and flashed it. All the color in the salesman's face washed out. Skylar spent the next thirty minutes test driving four vehicles with no intention of buying them just to annoy him for being a jerk. At the end when he asked if she was ready to buy she simply handed the keys over and told him not today, then turned and walked away.

Yep, the world was full of shady characters. People who would lie to avoid problems or simply to get what they wanted, the question was... what did Nancy want?

The truck coughed again, then black smoke started swirling out from under the hood, blocking her view of the road ahead.

"Goddammit." Skylar smashed her fists against the steering wheel as it came to a crawl and then the engine cut out. She hopped out and popped open the hood only to be enveloped by black smoke. Skylar waved a hand in front of her face trying to get a better look. "Ugh, I should have taken a cruiser," she said. Stepping away from the mess she placed a call to the local garage. She'd become a popular customer of theirs bringing the truck in on a monthly basis. They'd asked her why she wouldn't part with the truck and she would always tell them the same thing — there were sentimental reasons, and she wasn't lying. It had been given to her by her father, many years ago in what she believed was an attempt at trying to bridge the gap and mend the relationship between them. Back then it had been in good shape, but it was no match for New York winters. The salt started eating away at the metal and problems soon followed.

"Okay, thanks, Jim. Yeah. I'm just on Bay Avenue."

Deflated but determined to not lose her shit, she took

a seat on the grass near her truck and looked out across the bay. She wasn't far from the Moorings of Carrabelle and had considered walking back to her boat until she could get a ride back to the station to collect another vehicle.

As she sat there minding her own business, laying on her side in the shade and basking in the glorious sunshine, a black SUV pulled up and the window dropped. There beyond the glass with a smug grin on her face was Barb from the Carrabelle.

"Having a little trouble?"

"Nothing that the garage can't fix. How are you, Barb?"

"Oh living the dream. Living the dream," she said glancing away and lifting up her oversized sunglasses. "Do you need a ride?"

"Why, you offering?"

Barb smiled and shut off her engine. When she pushed out of her vehicle, Barb was wearing a pair of mom jeans pulled up to her belly button and a white blouse, along with flip flops. She had her hair up in a bun, and had dyed it a dark black.

"New hairdo?"

Barb patted the back of her hair like she was all pleased with it. "Yeah, you like it?"

"I preferred the full head of silver but hey, it might grow on me." Skylar tossed a piece of grass and smiled. She knew it would rile her up but that was the intention. After their last run-in they hadn't spoken to each other and Barb had made it clear that she was unwanted in her café. Childish? Of course it was but some folks were quite particular about where they expected residents to shop. Barb stood over her blocking out the sun.

"You mind?" she asked, motioning to the grass beside her.

"I don't know. I tend to prefer people sitting on the left of me," she said jokingly. Barb picked up on it and smiled and took a seat. She leaned back on her hands gazing up at the sun.

"Gorgeous day."

"That it is. What do you want, Barb?"

"Can't I sit here and just enjoy the weather?"

"Barb?" Skylar asked again knowing that she hadn't just stopped to chit-chat.

"Okay, rumor has it that Harvey was seen at the Vagabond."

"Seriously, Barb. Do you not have like a hobby or something to keep you interested? Surely all your time can't be spent on checking up on where people go to get their morning cup of joe?"

"Actually I was hoping you could pass on a message to Harvey."

"What, that he's banned from your establishment as well? At this rate you'll have no one left."

"I was going to say that I didn't mind. A friend of mine saw him down there and he said he was acting all nervous and worried. Let him know that it's fine."

"Why don't you?" Skylar asked.

"Because I have a feeling he won't come back out of fear of what I will say."

"Fear?" Skylar laughed. "You are talking about a grown ass man."

Barb cut her a look. "You really have no worries, do you?"

"Oh believe me I have my worries and based on the numerous conversations with you, Barb, I'm worried about your mental health."

She laughed which was quite the opposite of what Skylar thought she would do. She was used to her flying off the handle over the smallest remark. Barb picked a piece of grass and placed it between her lips like a cigarette and chewed on it a little. "I've been the only café in this town, or at least the only one that people have come to, for as long as I can remember. I admit, seeing Vagabond open up riled me up but since our last conversation—"

"Spat, you mean?"

"Call it that if you wish," Barb said. "But I realized that perhaps I've acted a little over the top."

"You think?" Skylar smirked looking up at the deep

blue sky and watching a cluster of clouds slowly drift by.

"Anyway, I have decided that I am going to reach out to Donnie Who."

"Donnie Wu," Skylar said, correcting her.

"Is that his name? Dear me, I've been calling him Donnie Who since he arrived. No wonder he gave me a strange look when I saw him today."

"Are you sure that wasn't your hairstyle he was reacting to?"

Barb nudged her and smiled. "I guess what I'm trying to say is that what matters to me most is the people. I'm just like anyone else, Skylar, I get jealous when new competition shows up in town, but I'm starting to see that perhaps it's a good thing. How can people really know what's good without the bad, right?"

"Are you suggesting Donnie's coffee is bad?"

"Of course not. Well, maybe just a little but that's for a customer to decide, not me."

Skylar looked at her. "You know what, Barb. I think Donnie would be pleased to hear you say that."

"Well let's not jump the gun here. I'm not going down there and telling him that, that's for sure. Oh no, but people like yourself, regular customers, yeah. It's time for some change."

"I'm pleased to hear you say that."

As they were talking the garage's tow truck came down the road.

"Ooh, that's me."

"Are you sure I can't give you a ride?" Barb asked.

Skylar looked at her then at Jim and raised a finger. "Give me a second to bring Jim up to speed and sure, I'll grab a lift. I appreciate that."

"It's the least I can do. And Skylar."

Skylar went to walk away.

"I'm sorry for how I treated you at the café."

Skylar knew that it took a lot for her to say that. "Hey, if I spoke out of line, I'm sorry too. Let's forget about it, huh?"

She nodded. Once she had given Jim the lowdown on her piece of junk and handed over the keys, she hopped into Barb's air-conditioned, brand-new SUV and headed back to the station to collect one of the cruisers.

* * *

Thirty minutes later she finally arrived outside Nancy's home. She pushed out and strolled up to the door looking around for the groundskeepers. She figured they would be out there trimming the grass and hedges to perfection but the place was quiet. Skylar gave a short knock on the door and waited. When she got no answer she tried again. She pressed the buzzer this time and moved around to the window and looked inside. She turned and noticed that her SUV wasn't in the driveway. Assuming that she might be in the rear, maybe taking a dip in the pool, she made her way around soaking in the sight of her well-landscaped property.

As she reached the rear, she noticed no one was in the pool. That's when she heard the sound of rustling, like tree leaves being crunched. She looked up at the large vine that covered the east side of the house and noticed someone climbing in through an open window. The bottom half of their body was hanging out while the rest of them was inside.

"Hey!" Skylar yelled. "What the hell are you doing up there?"

The person stopped moving, and she made her way over to the trellis. She placed her foot on it to see how sturdy it was. She wasn't overweight but she had her concerns about climbing up.

"You might want to climb back out. I'm from Franklin Sheriff's Office."

The person shuffled until they were closer to the window frame and then stuck their head out. It was a guy. "You don't look like a cop," he said.

Skylar held up her badge. "Come on down."

The guy looked to be late-teens. He had a full head of hair, short, spiky, and an athletic frame. He was wearing a baseball cap with the Florida Bobcats logo on the front, a Metallica T-shirt and ripped jeans. Once his boots hit the ground, Skylar stepped in and grabbed him by the wrist clamping a handcuff on one wrist before he could do anything.

"Who are you? And what are you doing breaking into Mrs. Hammond's house?"

"I'm her son."

"Son? But she didn't mention you."

"I doubt she would, I don't live with her," he said dropping his head. "Look, are you going to tell her about this?"

Skylar looked up at the window with a pinched brow. "Uh, let me think about that?" She paused for a second. "Yes. Now you want to tell me what's going on?"

"I forgot my key. Okay?"

"So you don't live with her but you have a key to her place?"

He nodded. "She lets me stay here on days when things aren't so good."

"So good?"

"With my father."

That's when the penny dropped. "So Nancy was previously married?"

"She was until a year ago. Her and my father didn't exactly get along."

"And where is your father's home?"

"Port St. Joe."

"You got ID on you?"

"Yeah in my front pocket."

"You got any syringes, a knife or anything that's liable to stick me?" Skylar asked before fishing into his pocket and pulling out his wallet. Once it was out she flipped it open and took a look at a school card. It had his image and date of birth. He had just turned eighteen and went by the name Conor Tamlin.

"Tamlin. Does your father own Tamlin Auto Salvage?"

"Yeah, you used it?"

She scoffed. "You could say that."

Jim's garage had given her a price on a new transmission for her truck a while back and she had considered it but decided it might be cheaper to find a used one and just pay to have them install it, so she'd called around to some of the auto salvages in the area —

Tamlin was one of them.

"How did you get here? I didn't see any vehicle out front."

He made a gesture with his head towards a cluster of pine trees near the back. There was a dirt bike leaning up against a tree.

"Nice bike."

"Just got it."

She nodded. "Shouldn't you be at school?"

He shrugged. "I don't go much."

"How come?"

"I'm going to work for my father once I'm out. I have a guaranteed job. It's the last year of school. What's the point?"

"There is always a point," she said. Skylar took the cuffs off him and he rubbed his wrist.

"You mind if I have a cigarette?" he asked.

"It's your lungs."

He snorted as he pulled out a pack and tapped one out.

Chapter 14

They walked to the porch at the back of the house and he took a seat. "So you heard about your mother's husband then, I gather?"

"I did," he said snapping his Zippo lighter shut and taking a hard drag.

"Did you get on with him?" Skylar asked.

"He was okay in small doses. I didn't like the way he treated my mother at times but then again I could say the same for my own father."

Skylar nodded and gazed out at the immaculate yard that had a water fountain that resembled an angel, a huge shed at the far end and a full-size swimming pool. What it must be like to have money, she thought.

"So what happened between your mother and father?"

"Nothing. Well, I mean they had their arguments like any couple do but she was swept up by Nick. I think because he was a lawyer she thought he had an endless stream of money."

Skylar gave a confused look. "But didn't she come into some money recently?"

"In the last six months. Yeah. But before that she didn't have two cents to rub together."

"But your father can't be exactly broke?"

"No he's not but he isn't rich either. Look, I love my mother but she has always cared more about what other people think than those in front of her. Being married to a lawyer. It carries a certain prestige, don't you think?"

"Maybe," Skylar replied. She contemplated what that might mean. If she was married to him for the prestige, why would she go to the trouble of killing him? If she'd come into money, again, why kill him? Something about it all didn't add up. Skylar glanced at her watch. The day was trailing away from her and she still had to speak with Nancy, and Keith.

"I'm guessing you know your mother is at work, right?"

He nodded.

"Where does she work?"

"A Cut Above. It's off the main stretch here in Apalachicola."

* * *

Wendy Owen's condo was crawling with cops. Harvey updated the lieutenant but hadn't managed to get a license plate off the vehicle. Fortunately surveillance caught it on camera and Miami police had put out an APB on the vehicle — though the chances of them finding it were slim to none. It had probably been stolen and was now in some ditch on fire.

Harvey glanced down at Wendy's lifeless body and shook his head.

"We were right here. This shouldn't have happened."

"You don't have eyes in the back of your head, detective," Lieutenant Moore said. "Trust me, if I came down on myself every time we let a suspect slip through our fingers, I'd be in a mental hospital."

That didn't make him feel any better. No doubt Davenport would hear about this and he'd add it to his long list of shortcomings. He groaned and stood up. Hanson came over and twisted a phone around. "We're in luck. I redialed the last number she phoned before she was shot and spoke to an older lady who lives about two miles north of here. Seems it's Bo's mother. While she doesn't want her son to get into trouble, she doesn't want him dead. She told us that he's stepped out but should be home in about half an hour."

"You got the address?"

"No, I hung up," Hanson said. "What do you think?" He laughed and so did the lieutenant. Harvey shook his head and made a beeline for the door. Hanson was quick to catch up. "Don't you think we should get in SWAT for this one?"

"Not unless you think mother dearest is planning on pulling out an AK-15," Harvey said jokingly.

"After what we just went through, that's not funny."

"We'll be fine."

"That's what you said on the way in here. Now look at this mess."

Chapter 15

Nancy was hard at work when Skylar walked through the door. A bell above let out a shrill and she glanced her way, then rolled her eyes. "What now?"

"Just a moment of your time."

"Can't you see I'm working?"

"So am I," Skylar replied.

Nancy turned to an African American woman. "Addison, can you take over here?" She then patted the customer on the arm. "I'll be right back." Nancy led the way into the rear where there was a small lunch room. It was cramped with just enough room for a table, two chairs, a sink and a small fridge. Nancy dropped down onto a chair and scooped up a pack of smokes. She lit up and blew smoke out the side of her mouth before crossing her arms.

"So?"

Skylar brought out her notepad and flicked through. "I

just wanted to confirm where you were on the night of Nick's death. Yeah, silly me I ended up scribbling down what you said but can't make head or tails of it."

She sighed.

"I finished work at five, went out for a drink with David Manning my boss and was home by six."

"And you never went out again that night?"

"Exactly."

"Strange, that must mean you have a doppelganger because cameras in the area picked you up entering Ruby's Bar an hour after your husband and then leaving before him. And the autopsy results show that your husband was actually poisoned using nothing more than common antifreeze, which I might add is readily available to anyone, including yourself."

She clenched her jaw and looked down at the ground for a second.

"Okay, I admit I was there but I didn't poison him."

"No? But you knew he was cheating on you. You knew there was a risk he might divorce you and then all that money that he'd been earning would go bye-bye."

"I told you. I didn't need his money. I had my own."

Skylar pushed away from the wall. "Ah yes, the inheritance. Your father, right?"

"Exactly."

Skylar stared at her. Even though they didn't have good surveillance of the inside, Nancy didn't know that. She was going to use a reverse tactic and pretend they did have it.

"And so why did you go there?"

She exhaled hard. "Look, Nick could be an ass but I loved him and I just couldn't keep repeating the same cycle of him going out after work and spending time with other women. I was going to give him an ultimatum."

"And did you?"

"Well you have surveillance, don't you?"

"Yeah we do but I'm curious to know why you didn't."

Skylar was reaching. It was very possible she did speak to him but call it a gut instinct she got a sense that at the last minute she decided not to.

"Because I didn't want to look like a fool. He'd already drunk too much and he was with someone."

"Keith?"

She nodded.

"So you were aware then of the situation that Keith placed your husband in?"

"Somewhat. My husband didn't share case files with me, if that's what you're asking?" She tapped her cigarette into the ashtray. A guy came into the room, he was dressed all spiffy looking in a bright green shirt, black pants and overly polished shoes.

"Any trouble, Nancy?"

"No, it's okay, David."

"Ah, David Manning, I presume?"

His brow pinched. "That's right. What's going on? Who are you?"

Skylar put out her hand. "Detective Reid. I'm sorry to hold up Nancy here but I just had a few questions for her. If you don't mind stepping out that would be great. Oh but don't go far, I've been meaning to get around to you and while I'm here I might as well kill two love birds with one stone."

David frowned.

"Oh, did I say love birds? I meant birds. Sorry."

He pursed his lips and exited the room. Skylar turned back to Nancy. "So I'm to believe that you went over there to confront him but nothing came of it."

"Exactly."

Skylar nodded. "Good-looking son you have."

Nancy straightened up in her seat.

"Oh I saw him at your house earlier. Yeah, I got quite a view as he tried to enter through a second-floor window. Surprising he didn't fall and break his neck."

"He was there?"

"Still is as far as I know."

She scooped up her phone and Skylar leaned on the table in front of her. "Keith White. What is your association to him?"

"He was a friend and client of Nick's."

"So you do know his clients. Do you know Bo Gonzales as well?"

"No. Nick brought Keith around a few times for dinner. They would smoke cigars in the parlor after supper and discuss business. I didn't really chat to him beyond small talk."

"But you saw him there that night," Skylar said.

"Where are you going with this?"

"It seems that it's possible that Keith might have had a motive for killing your husband. Do you recall Nick acting strange in the few months leading up to his death?"

"Nothing out of the usual. He worked hard. Drank harder and came in late. That was his pattern."

"And how did he view your son?"

"They chatted," she said then shrugged.

"Did they get on?"

"Of course they did."

"Strange, I got the sense that your son didn't like him."

She pulled another cigarette out, stubbed out what was

left of the last and fired up another. Nancy was obviously nervous. "Look, detective, my son wasn't exactly thrilled with me getting married to Nick. He loves his father Mike. He wanted me to stick around but there is a point when I had to make a decision for me. You can't stay in a loveless marriage," she said. Skylar thought about Jenna's relationship with Darryl.

"Do you know a guy named Darryl Harlow?"

"Never heard of him."

"Tattoos. He was there that night."

She shrugged. "There were a lot of people there that night. I hope you are following up with all of those because I would hate to see you wasting your time on me."

"Oh it's never a waste, Ms. Hammond. Nope. You'd be surprised what I learn from what is not said."

Nancy tapped more ash into the ashtray. "Look, are you going to arrest me?"

"Haven't decided yet. Lying to police, giving false information is a criminal offense. Section 837.05, Florida

Statutes. Yep. However, I might be prepared to overlook that if there was something, oh in the way of information you could provide about Keith White."

"What do you want to know?"

"Did you hear or see the argument between him and your husband?"

"No. I didn't. If they had one I left before that."

Skylar nodded. "Look I'm going to recommend you head on down to the police station and revise your statement. I would do it but it's probably best it comes from you. I think that will say a lot about you at a time when the eyes of justice are honing in you."

"Me? But I didn't do it. Okay I left out the part about me going to Ruby's but I had a good reason. I didn't want to be humiliated."

Skylar pulled a face and cocked her head to one side. "Humiliated."

"You live in Carrabelle, do you not, detective?"

"I do."

"Then you know how gossip can spread like a weed."

Skylar pursed her lips and nodded. "Reputation. Your son did say you cared a lot about what people thought of you."

As Skylar headed for the door, she cast a glance back. "By the way, how are things between you and your ex?"

"Good. As strange as it sounds we are on speaking terms. We have our moments but doesn't anyone who goes through a divorce?" She stubbed out her cigarette and got up. "Is that it? Are you not arresting me?"

Skylar looked out at the room full of hairdressers. As it stood they didn't have anything concrete on her beyond her leaving that part out of her alibi.

"That's it for now. Just don't go anywhere, okay? Oh and you might want to speak to your son."

With that said she walked out and made a motion with her head for David Manning to follow her outside. He was in the middle of doing his books. He laid his pen down and got up from the front desk and followed her. Skylar walked over to her cruiser and leaned against it.

"Which one is your vehicle?"

"What?"

"Your vehicle?"

David turned and pointed to a black Ford Escape. There wasn't a mark on the front end, and there were no other vehicles in the lot that were damaged. "Two nights ago, after work. Where were you?" Skylar asked.

"Out having a drink."

She looked at his hand and saw a wedding band. "Does your wife know?"

He looked back to his store. Nancy was looking out while working away on her client's hair.

"Well?" Skylar probed him deeper.

He sighed. "Look, we all have our relationship issues. The things we hide from those we love, and people we come to for a listening ear."

"So Nancy's your listening ear, is she? Or the one you love?"

He dropped his chin. "I was at the bar with Nancy, I then dropped her off at home around six."

"And then?"

"I went home."

"And you were in all night?"

"The ball game was on. So yeah."

"I'll need to confirm that. Can I get your wife's number?"

He got this real concerned look on his face. "You're not going to tell her about me and Nancy having a drink, are you? She wouldn't understand."

"I don't think many women would. Then again had you been out with a group maybe she wouldn't have anything to worry about."

He reached into a pocket, pulled out an old receipt and scribbled on the back a number for his house and handed it to her. "She hasn't been well. And Nancy was a listening ear. A friend. That's all. Think what you will, detective, but not everyone sleeps around on their wife."

"Are you referring to Nick?"

David pursed his lips and folded his arms. "If the boot fits." Skylar tapped the air with the receipt. "If everything checks out, my lips are sealed. You have my word."

Chapter 16

Ms. Gonzales was a widow living in a cramped mobile home in Bamboo Mobile Home Park just west of Pembroke Park. It was a quiet, tidy neighborhood filled with mostly elderly residents and blue-collar workers. Palm trees swayed in the breeze as they pulled up in the rental on Charles Road four homes down from Bo's place. They didn't want to spook him and they'd already told his mother that no harm would come to him if he came quietly. Unlike some mothers that Harvey had dealt with in the past, Bo's honestly seemed to care about his future. On the phone she kept repeating that he was a good kid but had fallen in with the wrong crowd. That kid was forty-six years old, certainly old enough to know right from wrong.

"You know he's going to be on the lookout," Hanson said. "Probably best if you go on down, and I'll wait here with the vehicle."

"Why?"

"That way if he bolts I can cut him off. If he drives out of here into that traffic we'll lose him."

"Ye of little faith," Harvey said tapping the steering wheel.

"Baker."

"Okay," he said throwing his hands up. Anything for a peaceful life. Harvey pushed out of the vehicle and Hanson slid on over. "Oh and if anyone offers you a drink, get one for me," he said.

Harvey looked back at him, one eyebrow rose. "Really?"

"What? I'm thirsty. It's hot out."

He shook his head as he walked away. Harvey approached the mobile home that was positioned at an angle. All of them were like that. Her home had an orange tree out front and the walkway and steps leading up to the front door were painted in bright red. With a blue door, cream-colored sides and white window it really was an eyesore. Harvey gave the door a knock with the back of his hand and stood back. A minute or two later a woman in her early seventies pushed open the screen door.

"Yes?"

"Ma'am, we spoke on the phone. Detective Baker."

"Oh yes, come on in."

She led the way inside and the first thing that caught his attention was the dank smell of weed. It was awful. The woman, who was around five ten in stature, and thin framed with a gaunt face, took a seat in front of the television. Some talk show was playing. She turned down the volume and eyed him as she reached for her cigarette from a tray that was already jam-packed with stubs and a half-eaten apple.

"He's not back yet but he shouldn't be long."

"Ms. Gonzales, how long has your son been here?"

"Several weeks. After that bitch took him for all his money he didn't have a place to stay. I don't have much room here but as long as I'm breathing he will always have a roof over his head."

Harvey nodded scanning the room. There were several framed photos on the counter. She must have caught him staring as she said, "That's him when he was fourteen. He was a wild kid and tended to run with the wrong crowd at times but he has a heart of gold. He'd never harm anyone."

"Is that so?" Harvey said. Parents could be naïve at times. How many criminals had disappointed their mothers? How many would have been ashamed to have their parents know what they had done while chasing the green? Harvey would have taken a seat on the sofa but it was covered with stacks of old newspapers, piles of laundry and dirty dishes that she obviously hadn't got around to cleaning.

"How's he been since the divorce?"

"Down in the dumps. Besides the odd visit to the store he rarely comes out of his room. He sits with me and plays cards but lately it's been getting less frequent. What was this you said about his ex-wife dead?"

"Yeah, that's why I'm here to see him."

"You don't think he's responsible, do you?"

"No, we know who did it. I mean, we can identify them but we don't have names. I thought he might be able to shed some light on it."

"He—"

Before she could finish the front door opened and in came Bo with two bags of groceries in his hands. "I got the fruit you wanted, Ma..." His eyes bounced from her to Harvey and then he dropped the bags and bolted out the door.

"Bo!" his mother cried out at the same time as Harvey. Not wasting a second, Harvey raced after him, bursting out into the sunshine only to have a flower pot thrown at him. It smashed on the ground and Bo took off down the road heading in the direction of Hanson. Harvey didn't need to indicate to him, he was already ready. As Bo came running down the road, he glanced back to see where Harvey was and wasn't paying attention to the driver's door that had been opened. There was a loud thud as his body collided with it and he hit the ground. Hanson was on him quickly, flipping him onto his front and slapping cuffs on him just as Harvey came rushing up out of breath.

"I didn't do anything."

Hanson hauled him to his feet and pushed him up against the SUV while reading him his rights and checking his pockets for any weapons or drugs. He squirmed in Hanson's grasp.

"Settle down," Harvey said placing a hand on his shoulder and keeping him against the SUV. Hanson pulled out of his pockets and placed on the hood of the SUV, one pack of Marlboro Lights, a lighter, forty dollars, some loose change and a stick of gum. "Are you aware that your ex-wife was murdered today?"

He turned his head, a look of shock, perhaps bewilderment spread across his face. "That's impossible."

"Well it's happened. She's dead. We are going to bring you in to see if you can identify the men that were caught on camera fleeing the scene."

"They didn't work for me, if that's what you're

insinuating."

"I didn't say they did."

"They are probably from the Outlaws group." He then looked real worried. "How did you get this address?"

"You ex-wife. It was the last number she dialed but I'm guessing your mother didn't tell you that."

"I was out," he replied before Hanson led him around to the back of the vehicle and put him inside. Harvey turned at the sound of his mom's voice. Harvey waved to her and told her that there was nothing to worry about. They were going to question him down at the station and they would keep her updated. That obviously didn't cut it as she shuffled down the road telling them to wait.

Harvey remained outside the vehicle while Hanson got in to keep an eye on Bo.

"Ms. Gonzales, I'm going to give you my card. If you have any questions contact this number but right now it's probably best you go back inside and leave this to us."

She tapped on the window. "Is there anything you need?"

"Mom, just go in," Bo said looking mortified by the whole experience. Several of the neighbors had come out to gawk. Bo's mother turned to head back and told them to mind their own business. That was one fiery lady.

Chapter 17

"What did you do with all that money?" Skylar asked Keith White. After finishing up with Nancy she'd headed back to the department to find out why he'd lied to them.

"I told you it's gone. I don't have it anymore," he said from across the table in the interview room. Skylar glanced at the one-way mirror. Behind it were Reznik and Davenport. She hated conducting interviews in front of people, especially top brass.

"I realize that. What did you spend it on?"

"The casinos in Miami. Some of the money was used to get my business off the ground, the rest was spent down at the casinos."

"Strange. According to Wendy Owen you paid them back every cent except for the last time you got a loan."

"Who said that?"

"Oh don't play that card. You know full well. She was married to Bo Gonzales."

"Oh, that Wendy."

Skylar shook her head, she could tell he was holding back.

"Look." He stared at the one-way mirror then back at Skylar. "I had a string of good luck. You know when I first went to Bo and got a loan it was just for my business. I paid it back, and then I got into visiting casinos and well you know how things go. I hit a bad patch and needed more money to feed my addiction. Bo was there. They always gave me money. I started winning back and it seemed like I couldn't fail. I would go in there with a couple of thousand and come out with double the amount but then I would blow through my winnings. Yeah, I know what they were saying down at Rapid Loans. That I had some gig going but the fact was I was winning and losing. I just happened to be on a very good winning spree and I decided to go big."

"How much?"

"Two hundred thousand."

"Um, that's a fair chunk of change," Skylar said.

"I lost it all. That's why I gave Nick the tape. It was insurance to make sure that if they found me I had something over him but he went and used it to help Wendy."

"That must have burned you, especially when you found out that he was seeing Wendy on the side."

"Why would that bother me?"

"Come on, Keith. Do you want to walk down that road? Wendy told us all about you stalking her, sending flowers, even coming on to her. You were obsessed with the woman."

He went red in the face.

"So let me go out on a limb here. I think you showed up at Ruby's Bar not just to confront Nick about handing over the tape. You were pissed because he was seeing Wendy and playing around with other women. So let me guess, you poisoned him then left thinking that would be enough, but it wasn't, was it? When you saw him come out, you drove him off the edge of the road hoping his vehicle would go into the bay but it didn't. Then you didn't stick around because maybe someone came by. How am I doing?" Skylar asked.

"You are way off!" He leaned forward. "I admit I gave him the tape, and I was pissed at him for going behind my back and seeing Wendy but I wouldn't kill him for that. You have to be insane."

"Wendy thinks you are."

He snorted and shook his head. "You can't keep me here. You have nothing on me. I want my lawyer now!"

Skylar tapped the table. "Yeah that might take a while being as your last one is dead."

The door opened. It was Davenport. He jerked his head to indicate he wanted to speak with her. Skylar got up and smiled at Keith. Criminals would say and do anything to get out of jail. He was no different.

Outside, once the door was closed, Davenport told her to walk with him.

"Just leave it now."

"But sir, we are so close. He had the means, the motive and the opportunity."

"So did a lot of people in that place. It's not enough, Reid." He took a deep breath. "Anyway, Harvey just got back in touch. They've managed to track down Bo Gonzales, and Wendy Owen is dead."

"Dead?" She stared back blankly. "Is Bo responsible?"

"That's what they're trying to establish. I think we can rule out Keith because he's been in here and unfortunately, Skylar, we did some digging around, Reznik has located footage of Keith at Magic City Casino and they have been able to confirm that he blew through thousands of dollars. He's telling the truth, Skylar."

"But that doesn't mean he isn't responsible for killing him. Desperation, jealousy, those can lead people to do all manner of things."

"Yeah but his vehicle doesn't have any damage on it. So unless he used another vehicle and unless we can find some connection beyond him being at Ruby's on the night, all we have is circumstantial."

She nodded. "I'm going to get in touch with Axl to see if he can go back over that footage inside the club. It was grainy. Maybe he can clean it up and work his magic on it. In the meantime, we should have Reznik speak with everyone down at the bar."

"Already done it," he said coming around the corner and joining them. "They all have solid alibis, and the camera across the street at the seafood restaurant confirms that none of the staff including the owner left that bar until a good forty minutes after our victim was dead."

Skylar paced then her phone rang. She stuck up a finger to let them know she would be right back and then walked a short distance away. It was the garage.

"Alright, Jim, hit me with the bad news," she said.

"Actually it's not too bad. You just need an engine thermostat. That's why your engine was overheating. I can get another one in but it's going to be a couple of days, or I can search around a few of the auto salvage yards. What do you want me to do?"

"You know what, leave it with me. I have to make a run over to Tamlin Auto Salvage to speak with the owner. I'll see if they have one in stock. If they do I'll drop it off."

"You know I can have them send it over."

"But you're going to add an additional cost for that and I'm trying to save money."

"I hear you. Okay, well give me a shout and if he has one I should be able to get it fixed up for you within the hour. Seriously though, Skylar, you should consider purchasing a new vehicle."

"New? I couldn't afford that."

"C'mon, you cops get paid more than us."

"At the prices you charge?" she asked then chuckled. "Oh by the way, Jim. Have you had anyone come in over the last few days with the front end of their vehicle banged up?"

"Uh let me check." He put the phone down and she could hear him tapping on keys. When he came back he didn't have good news. "Nope. Sorry."

"All right, thanks." She ended the call. Skylar went back to where Davenport and Reznik were shooting the breeze. "Listen, I'm heading over to Apalachicola to

Tamlin Auto Salvage. Reznik, do you think you can call around to some of the other local garages and see if any of them have had a vehicle come in with a front-end collision? I'm thinking whoever did this has to have some damage to their vehicle."

"I'm way ahead of you. That was one of the first things I looked into this morning. There was nothing," Reznik replied.

Chapter 18

Harvey turned around a tablet and slid it across the table in the interview room. On the screen was a zoomed-in image of the two men that had opened fire at the condo. "You recognize these two?"

Bo squinted then nodded. "Yeah, they work for Brent Rutz. They're part of the biker club." He sighed as he looked back up at him. "Was it quick? Wendy's death I mean?"

Harvey nodded. "Yeah."

He looked down and shook his head. "I never wanted this to happen. She kept harping on at me to get out of it but you know how it is when the money starts flowing, it's hard to pull away. I'd told her that we'd give it another year and then relocate out west or somewhere in Europe."

"A little too late."

Bo nodded looking despondent.

"How many times did you visit Carrabelle?"

"Twice. The first time I came looking for Keith, I couldn't find him. He'd closed his business and as far as I know he didn't have any family around these parts. Anyway, I got in touch with Darryl Harlow and asked him to keep an eye out for Keith being as he lived there."

"How long have you known him?"

"Darryl? He's an old buddy of mine. We go way back."

"So that's how you made the connection with the Outlaws?"

He took a swig of his coffee and nodded. "Yeah. It was a long time ago when he was running with them. Darryl was actually the one that pitched the idea to me of opening a loan shop. The Outlaws wanted a way to launder money from the drug business and what better way than to give it out to people who needed money and make some back. It was an investment on their part. I made the largest portion of the interest and they took a cut from it."

"So how did you know to return to Carrabelle?"

"Darryl was down at Ruby's. Guy can drink like a fish. Anyway he calls me up and tells me Keith was asking around for that lawyer friend of his. So I made my way up. We watched him for a day and then made our move to grab him but he managed to escape. Then a buddy of mine said he'd shown up down at Ruby's again."

"So you went down to confront him."

"Both of them. I thought I would kill two birds with one stone."

"Kill?"

"Figuratively I mean. I didn't kill him. In fact by the time we got there Keith was gone."

"Do you know what vehicle he was driving?"

"Yeah, it was a blue Chevy truck."

Harvey made a few notes. "And what else?"

"Nothing else. I got up in the face of that asshole lawyer and tried to get him to spill the beans on where Keith had gone. You know, he didn't even recognize me. Can you believe that? He ruined my life and he didn't even know what I looked like."

"Theoretically, Keith did but, yeah I get the point," Harvey said tapping his pen against the pad of paper in front of him. "So did you stick around?"

"I was kicked out. I'm sure you already know that. We caught a taxi back to Darryl's home and I left for Miami late that evening."

"So you didn't stick around to follow Mr. Hammond and drive his vehicle off the road?" Harvey asked.

"I don't own a vehicle."

"Then how did you get around Miami?"

"I had several drivers. Strange as it might sound I never got my driver's license."

"Are you kidding me?"

"I never wanted to drive a car."

"But everyone does," Harvey said.

"Well I'm not everyone."

"So you caught a taxi to the airport."

"Nope."

"So who was it in Carrabelle that drove you back to

the airport? Because I'm pretty sure Darryl wouldn't have been in a state to do it."

"A friend of mine."

"And his name is?" Harvey asked. He paused over the paper, ready to scribble it down.

Bo shook his head. "Not saying."

"Bo, you do realize the situation you are in, right?"

"I'm not getting him involved in this as he had nothing to do with this."

"Well then tell me. Is he local or from Miami?"

Bo looked around the room like he was done having the conversation. Harvey tried to reason with him and make it clear that he was facing some considerable jail time if tried to obstruct justice.

"Is it the same guy that alerted you to Keith being at the bar?"

"I've told you everything. I want a lawyer."

"You're going to need more than that," Harvey said gathering together his papers as he got up to leave and place a call to Franklin County Sherriff's Office.

Chapter 19

Reznik felt like a headless chicken running around doing Skylar's bidding. Go here, go there, check this out. Would you like me to tap dance as well, he felt like saying to her. And if that wasn't enough now Baker was adding in his two cents.

"Keith White is supposed to own a blue Chevy truck. Do you know what he was driving when he was seen pulling away from Ruby's Bar that night?"

"Yeah, hold on one second, I have Reid on the other line asking me to do the cha-cha as well."

"What?"

He groaned. "I'm kidding. Hold on a second."

He went over to his computer and brought up the copy of video footage taken from the CCTV across the street. "A gold sedan. White was driving a gold Toyota."

"Then we need to find this blue Chevy. It's very possible he's dumped it or has it parked somewhere."

"Would you like me to go and ask him?"

"Yeah, go do that," Harvey replied.

"What's the magic word?"

"What?"

"The magic word."

"Reznik. Do your job. That's the magic word," Harvey said and hung up. Reznik sat there with the phone pressed to his ear. He wasn't impressed with his attitude and he certainly didn't like being bossed around. It was one thing to take it from Davenport, even Hanson, but he was no puppet on a string.

"Who was on the phone?" Davenport asked, causing Reznik to spin around in his chair.

"Um. It was Harvey."

"What's he want?"

He updated him and Davenport drove home the need to find out where White was storing this blue truck. Reznik trudged down to his cell and flipped the flap down on the door. Inside Keith was walking back and forth.

"Am I getting out? Is my lawyer here?"

"Soon. Soon."

"That's what they told me four hours ago. I swear I'm going to file a civil lawsuit against this department. Shabby police officers. Crappy coffee. What is this world coming to?"

"Keith, where is the blue Chevy?"

"What?"

"The Chevy."

He stared back, looking reluctant to tell him so Reznik said, "Okay, see you in another four hours." He dropped the flap, smiled and waited a few seconds and then heard Keith banging on the other side. "Officer. Hey!"

Reznik dropped the flap. "Yes?"

"Okay, okay. I can't take being in here any longer. Look, I store it over at TTC Storage. It's on Hatfield Street in Eastpoint."

"Thank you kindly," Reznik said closing the flap.

"Hey. When am I getting out of here?" Reznik walked away to the sound of banging on the door.

Chapter 20

Tamlin Auto Salvage yard was an absolute dump. It was a skeleton graveyard full of steel bones, and stacks of used tires. Skylar pulled onto the property and parked outside the head office. There were vehicles for as far as the eye could see. Fortunately the place was shrouded in trees and set back off Industrial Road just northeast of the town.

Skylar pushed out of the cruiser and made her way into the poorly air-conditioned front office. It stank of grease and oil and looked as if it hadn't seen a cleaning cloth in over a decade. Off to her left was a small waiting area with chairs that looked as if they'd seen better days. One was stained with something brown. She didn't want to know what that was. There was an empty five-gallon water jug machine, and a small table covered in ripped auto magazines. Off to her right was a small cabinet with trophies for baseball. Skylar approached the cabinet and saw that Conor's name was engraved at the bottom of a trophy. Obviously his father took great pride in his kid, enough to display him front and center in his business.

"Can I help you?"

She turned, slightly startled by the appearance of a man in dirty blue overalls wiping his greasy hands on a cloth. He was wearing a dirty baseball cap and had a cigarette sticking out the corner of his mouth.

"Would Mike be around?"

"Who's asking?"

She pulled her badge out and he nodded. "I'm Mike."

"Strange, I was in here a few months back, and didn't see you around. There was a woman…"

"Judith. Yeah she usually mans the counter but she's off today. How can I help you?"

"I'm here about the death of Nick Hammond."

"Oh him."

"Do you mind telling me where you were two nights ago?"

He reached for a can of soda pop on the counter and

took a swig of it before hopping up onto a chair. That's when Skylar noticed he had a limp.

"You hurt yourself?" she asked.

He looked down. "It's a prosthetic leg," Mike said pulling up the pant leg to show her. "I did two combat tours. The last one I wasn't so lucky."

"Right. Thanks for serving our country."

"Appreciate that. There aren't many who seem to care." He sighed then answered her question. "Two nights ago I was out on a friend's boat. I can give you his name if you like. There were four of us there and they can vouch for me."

She nodded as he went about searching for his phone. He pulled it out and handed it over. Skylar took down the name and number.

"You ever had any run-ins with Nick?" she asked as she jotted it down.

"Nope. He stayed clear of here and I never went over there."

"But Conor did."

"Conor misses his mom. He always has. Things didn't work out well between us but he's a good kid and that's about the only thing Nancy and me agree on. He's out back getting vehicles ready for crushing if you want to speak to him"

"No, it's okay, I spoke to him already. Seems like a bright lad. Nice bike he has."

"Oh the Kawasaki?" He snorted. "Yeah, I gave him heck over that purchase."

"Cost too much?"

"That and the fact that he ruined a good vehicle."

"Oh, he banged up his last one?"

"You could say that. Yeah."

Skylar looked around. "Would you have an engine thermostat?"

"We have a lot of them," he said jerking his head to the yard.

"It's for a 1984 Ford F-250."

"Whoa, don't see many of those around nowadays."

"No you don't," she replied.

"Sentimental?" he asked.

She smiled. "Exactly. Some people don't get it."

"I have a '76 Chevy Impala. It used to belong to my dad." He turned to his computer. "Let me see what I can find." He fired up the laptop in front of him and started tapping in the details.

"You got a washroom?"

He made a waving gesture to a rear door. "Just out back, last door on the right."

She walked down a narrow corridor and entered the bathroom, if it could even be called that. The trash can was overflowing with paper towels, the floor was soaked in urine and someone hadn't flushed the toilet. It also didn't help that they were out of toilet paper rolls.

As she was contemplating using it, her phone started ringing. She grimaced looking around as she made her way back out into the corridor. She fished around for her phone and walked out the back door into the yard to take the call.

"Axl, how did you get on?"

"Well I managed to clear up the footage. It's not great but it's better than what was there. I lightened it and adjusted levels and I have something for you."

"Let's hope it's good as right now we are spinning wheels, literally."

She glanced out across the yard and spotted Conor in one of the large cranes. He fired it up and a huge arm turned to a massive pile of vehicles.

"Well here's the thing. Even though it was hard to see in the original video, after I enhanced it and zoomed in, I got Ms. Hammond on video inside."

"Nice, does she head over and speak to Nick?"

"No, that's the strange part. The video captures her walking in, and looking around and then she makes her way over to the bar area and chats to someone. It looks like a guy. It's hard to see who he is because his back was turned away from the bar. However, after a few minutes of talking, the guy walks out and gets into a red truck. I managed to get a partial license plate off it but I was going to check this alongside the video that Reznik got from the seafood place."

"Good. And what about Nancy?"

"She remained at the bar for one drink and then she left."

"Without speaking with Nick?" Skylar asked.

"Yeah. Okay hold on, I'm at Reznik's desk and just pulling up the footage now."

"Where is he?"

"Oh he headed off to some storage facility in Eastpoint. Apparently Keith has a blue Chevy truck. They want to see if the front end is damaged."

As Axl mumbled away to himself while bringing up the footage, Skylar made her way through the maze of steel towards Conor.

"I must have a word with Reznik about his computer. You should see how many icons he has on the desktop. It's a mess."

"What was that license plate, Axl?" Skylar asked squinting into the distance as the large crane clamped on to a red truck and began raising it.

"938 X. The last two letters were out of view of the bar's camera but hopefully... Oh, here we go. Give me a second."

As Skylar got closer to the crane, Conor looked out and gave a short wave. She smiled and lifted a hand.

"There it is. 938 XQG. It's a red Ford truck."

Skylar glanced up at the crane's huge arm as it brought over the red truck to a steel crushing machine. She squinted as it moved past her line of sight and that's when she saw it. "938 XQG," she blurted out.

"That's right, that's it," Axl said.

"I'm looking at it."

"What?"

"Hey! Conor!" Skylar yelled but he couldn't hear her because he had on an ear protection headset. She pulled out her service weapon and fired two shots into the air. That got his attention. He twisted around and she made a gesture for him to cut the engine. He looked as if he was having difficulty hearing. All the while the crane's arm kept moving until it was poised over the crushing machine. The claw released and the red truck dropped down into the machine.

Without wasting another second, Skylar broke into a sprint heading for the machine. She could already hear it beginning to engage as large massive steel jaws started to close in on the vehicle.

Skylar darted across the muddy property and slammed her hand against a red emergency stop button causing the whole unit to switch off. Panting and doubled over trying to catch her breath she looked back at Conor who was now getting down from the crane. Skylar climbed up the side of the crushing machine and looked inside.

Sure enough, there it was.

The front end had been busted up, the right headlight was gone but the most important thing still remained — streaks of green paint that had been transferred when it had struck Nick Hammond's vehicle.

Chapter 21

Eight hours later

For all the murder cases that Skylar had been assigned to, one thing she'd come to realize was that not all of them were complicated to solve. Some hid the evidence, others left it in plain sight, and others went to great lengths to avoid detection, however in this case it turned out the motive was simple.

"Hold on a second, you're telling me it wasn't Conor or his father?" Harvey said perched on the edge of Skylar's desk.

"No. It was Nancy. Of course she wasn't going to come out with it but once we dragged her son into the station, she admitted it."

"What we will do for our kids. So what, she was jealous?"

"Yeah, it wasn't money. This truly was a case of where someone was in a relationship for all the wrong reasons.

Nancy might have had her suspicions that Nick was cheating on her but because she loved him or was in love with the prestige that came from being married to a lawyer and living in a well-to-do neighborhood she looked the other way. Unfortunately her son Conor couldn't do that. He was the one that discovered footage on Nick's phone of him with another woman. He showed it to his mother and tried to convince her to leave him and go back to Mike. Nancy refused but said she would deal with it in her own way. Well it seems that she did."

"By poisoning him."

Skylar took a bite of her apple and rocked back and forth in her chair while nodding. "Yeah, she topped off his drink at home with it, thinking it would kill him off and wouldn't be detected because it was a form of alcohol. The only problem is…"

"It is detectable," Harvey said.

"Yeah, and as death can occur within twenty-four hours after ingestion, it didn't take long for it to shut down Nick's system."

"So you think she gave it to him before he went out that evening."

Skylar nodded. "And she knew he would drink more. She figured the police would focus on the bar not her."

"So why did she go to the bar?"

"Well that's where it gets a little convoluted. That guy you were searching for, the friend of Bo, who told him Keith was at the bar, and the one who picked him up later that evening to go to the airport. It was Conor."

"Hold on a second. You are saying that Conor knew him?"

"It appears when he was snooping through Nick's belongings he didn't just uncover the video of him cheating but he came across the case Nick was working on with Wendy and Bo and the video. He figured that if his mother didn't do anything he would. He got in contact with Bo and told him about Nick, and Keith's relationship and said that he could hand both of them on a platter to him."

Harvey's brow pinched. "Holy crap."

"On Conor's phone. It's all in text messages between the two of them."

"So that's why he didn't want to mention him. He was protecting the kid."

"A kid that's eighteen and responsible for his actions," Skylar said. "He showed up at Ruby's Bar that night to keep an eye on Keith and to confront Nick when Bo turned up but Keith slipped out."

"Conor didn't see him leave?"

"No, Conor wasn't there by that point. We have him on surveillance. When his mother showed up, she told him to go home. To leave it and that she'd take care of it."

"Poisoning him."

Skylark nodded. "You see one of the effects of having consumed antifreeze is that a person might appear drunk. And I recall the bartender saying that when Nick rolled in he was already acting like he'd drunk one too many but according to Nancy, he only had one drink at dinner with his meal."

"The one she poisoned."

"Exactly. Then it was just a matter of time before his internal organs shut down."

Harvey got off the desk. "The lengths people will go. So Conor didn't listen to his mother and she probably didn't tell him that she'd poisoned Nick, so he took matters into his own hands and drove him off the road."

"Bingo!" Skylar said. "Except he didn't stick around to watch the curtains close."

"And she admitted to this?"

"Like I said, not initially but she did it to protect her boy from being accused of murder."

"And yet he's still going to be arrested for attempted murder."

Skylar nodded. "Look, I got to head out. I said I would meet with Ben. He's home now and he wanted to chat. I should get going."

She walked backwards thumbing over her shoulder.

"Hold on a second, you didn't tell me what happened with Reznik and Keith's vehicle," Harvey said.

"Oh, right, yeah, the blue Chevy was there. No damage to the front. Obviously."

"But why was he storing it there?"

"It had two hundred thousand zipped up in a bag in the trunk."

Harvey smiled. "That old dog. He did have it."

"Did, would be the correct word," Skylar said winking at him before exiting the building.

* * *

Twenty minutes later she turned off her engine outside Ben's home. It was nearly dark out, the air was thick and humid and she was looking forward to crawling back into her boat and returning to a world without murder — even if it would only be for a few days.

Small lights illuminated the outside of his home as she walked up to the door to knock. Before she did, the door opened up and Ben came out. He was wearing a blue shirt, white shorts, and a pair of Nike sneakers.

"Well, hey there, stranger," Skylar said clasping her hands behind her back.

Ben pulled the door closed. "Thanks for coming."

"No problem. How's Sam?"

He shrugged. "He's fine." He motioned for them to talk by her cruiser. The truck wouldn't be repaired for a while because after she arrested Conor, his father naturally didn't want to do business with her.

"You want to go get a drink, maybe a bite to eat?" she asked assuming everything was okay.

"No. I..." He pursed his lips together and looked past her as if he was trying to find the words. "Look, please don't take this the wrong way. I appreciate you stepping in at the last minute and looking after Sam but..." He frowned. "Teaching him to fight. That's what you thought would help him?"

Skylar was a bit taken aback by the tone. "Look, I just thought that if he knew how to protect himself he might not end up coming home with a black eye or skipping out of school."

"The school has suspended him."

"What? No, that can't be."

"You wanted them to deal with bullying. Well they just did."

"But I told the school that if they tried playing that card I would..."

He put a hand up to cut her off. "You would do what? Huh? Arrest them? I'm the one that has to deal with this on a daily basis. I'm the one that has to show up there every day. You only needed to do it for two days. Now he's confused. You were telling him to fight back. I'm telling him that's not the way and the school now has him in their crosshairs as a bully."

Skylar opened her mouth but before she could get a word in edgeways he put up a finger. "No, before you justify your actions like you always do, let's be clear here — you have only made the situation worse."

Skylar saw Sam looking out of the window.

"Okay. I'm sorry. I didn't intend to make your life hard."

"Well you did."

Her brow furrowed. "Ben."

"I know you were trying to do what you think is right but it didn't help. You're not his mother, Skylar. Leave the parenting to me."

With that said he turned and walked back into his home leaving her there speechless. Sam disappeared from the window but not before quickly waving. Skylar remained there for a few more minutes second-guessing herself and chewing over his words. Skylar climbed back into her cruiser with a heavy heart and turned over the engine. She thought about going back and apologizing again but she figured she'd done enough damage. That evening she returned to her empty boat and for the first time since arriving in Carrabelle she felt a longing to return to the city. Skylar scooped up her phone and made a phone call to an old friend, the one person who could lift her spirit.

A few seconds later he answered.

"Scot," she said.

"Hey, you. You keeping out of trouble?"

She blew out her cheeks. "More like creating it."

"Uh oh, I'm guessing all that therapy isn't working."

She chuckled and over the next hour sat on the edge of the boat looking across the bay, drinking a beer and chatting as the final streaks of red disappeared beyond the horizon. A light breeze blew in causing waves to lap and a distant harbor bell rang out. Life in Carrabelle was very different to the big city, it had taught her a lot in a short time but most of all it had shown her that it wasn't always sunshine and rainbows, you had to be prepared to weather the storms, and she could feel a storm brewing, deep inside her.

* * *

THANK YOU FOR READING

Dead Drop Book 4

Book 5 is coming soon.

Please can you leave a review, even if it's just 10 words.

A Plea

Thank you for reading DEAD DROP. If you enjoyed the book, I would really appreciate it if you would consider leaving a review. Without reviews, an author's books are virtually invisible on the retail sites. It also lets me know what you liked. You can leave a review by visiting the book's page. I would greatly appreciate it. It only takes a couple of seconds.

Thank you — **Emma Rose Watts**

Newsletter

Thank you for buying Dead Drop: Coastal Suspense Series Book 4 published by Coastal Publishing.

Click here to receive special offers, bonus content, and news about new Emma Rose Watts books. Sign up for the newsletter. http://www.emmarosewatts.com/

About the Author

Emma Rose Watts is the not so cozy pen name of the bestselling cozy mystery author Emma Watts. Under the name Emma Rose Watts, she writes gritty suspense and mysteries based in Florida. She is from Maine. She is married, and has kids and a dog.

Made in the USA
Middletown, DE
30 September 2018